The case of [illegible] ...wn to the press, [illegible] ...e public in Se[illegible] month a wom[illegible] a few miles ou[illegible] ...ales. She was dressed in [illegible] ...crepe oriental-style pyjamas, decor[illegible] ...with a green dragon motif. The thighs and buttocks had been exposed and the head covered with a badly scorched sack. When this was removed it revealed that a white towel edged with blue and red was wrapped around the head, which had been smashed in with a heavy, blunt instrument. Apart from being bludgeoned, she had also been shot in the side of the head.

FATAL PASSIONS

Adrian Vincent

WARNER BOOKS

A *Warner* Book

First published in Great Britain in 1992
by Macdonald
This edition published 1992 by Warner

Copyright © 1992 Adrian Vincent

The moral right of the author has been asserted.

A CIP catalogue record for this book
is available from the British Library.

ISBN 0 7088 4996 2

Printed and bound in Great Britain by
Cox & Wyman Ltd, Reading

Warner Books
A Division of
Little, Brown and Company (UK) Limited
165 Great Dover Street
London SE1 4YA

CONTENTS

THE LOVE BUNGALOW

Patrick Mahon

English murder case 1924

Patrick Mahon was a good-looking man with a ready and charming smile which could have a devastating effect on a susceptible young girl or a lonely unmarried woman past her prime. He had devoted much of the last fourteen years of his life to the relentless pursuit of such women, all totally deceived by his comforting and reassuring manner which gave them the feeling they were in safe hands. Nothing, of course, was further from the truth – as poor Emily Kaye was to find out. The cold-blooded way he killed her, and the manner in which he disposed of the body, arrays him alongside such an infamous killer as George Smith, who sat down to play *Nearer my God to Thee* on the harmonium immediately after he had killed his wife in her bath.

A Liverpool Irishman, Patrick Mahon was brought up in nearby West Derby, and seems to have led a blameless life until he was twenty, when he married. Having discovered sex through his marriage, there was no stopping him. His first known conquest was a young woman whom he took for a weekend on the Isle of Man, paid for by a series of forged cheques – a petty crime for which he was arrested, and was lucky to get off with nothing more than being bound over. Instead of learning his lesson, Mahon embarked on a career of crime which included embezzlement and fraud, culminating in robbery with violence when he knocked a servant girl unconscious with a hammer when she interrupted him robbing a house. By the time he was thirty-four, the good Catholic boy who had been a regular churchgoer had become a liar, a thief

3

and an ex-con who had gone down for five years for robbery with violence.

We have no record of what Mrs Mahon's feelings were while her husband was busy building himself a reputation for being a violent and habitual criminal. One can only assume that she was a meek and passive woman prepared to endure anything to keep the home intact. But loyal to her man she certainly was, and she remained so until that fateful day when she found the cloakroom ticket that was to send Patrick Mahon to the gallows.

When Mahon came out of prison, he found his wife waiting for him in their home in Richmond, Surrey, where they had been living for a number of years. One of their two children had died while he was in prison, and his homecoming was therefore not the happiest of reunions. But at least his wife had a job in Sunbury, with a firm marketing soda fountains. Thanks to her influence, Mahon was appointed as the company's sales manager, which says much for her loyalty to her husband but little for the company's security controls.

At this stage it would have been quite easy for Mahon to abandon his old ways and become a respectable citizen for the first time in his married life. He now had a well-paid job, a reasonable home and a loyal, supportive wife. And for some time he did try. He did his job well and became a member of the Richmond Bowling Club, where he seems to have been well liked by his fellow bowling enthusiasts. If his job had not taken him to the offices of Robertson, Hill and Company in the City, he could well have ended his days in obscurity, contenting himself with the occasional affair until he was too old to be attractive to women. As it was, when he visited the company he met Emily Kaye, an attractive single woman of thirty-eight, who worked there as a secretary. That fatal meeting was to have dire consequences for both of them.

They were attracted to each other from the start, though he saw her as no more than just another conquest to be discarded as soon as he had become bored. Emily, on the other hand, fell madly in love and saw him as a potential husband, even though she knew that he was already married. In no time at all they were on intimate terms.

After they had been sleeping together for some time, Emily decided one afternoon to make her feelings and intentions clear while they were in bed in her bed-sitting room in the Green Cross Club in Guildford Street, which she shared with a woman named Eileen Warren. 'Patrick,' she said, 'you do love me, don't you?'

'Of course,' he said absently, his mind more occupied with finding an explanation for his continual late arrivals home – he was sure his wife had already begun to suspect that another woman had appeared on the horizon.

'And do you mean it, when you say you're no longer in love with your wife?'

'You know that's true.' He stared up at the ceiling, his mind suddenly alert as he became aware that they were moving into deep waters.

'Then why don't you leave her?'

He sighed. 'There's the child to think about, dear.'

But Emily was not so easily deflected from the course of action she had decided was right for both of them. 'The child would probably be better off without you,' she told him. There then followed one of those highly charged dialogues which errant husbands often experienced, generally ending up with the man promising to do something about it when the right moment came up to speak of divorce.

'Why don't you just leave?' Emily said. 'We could go abroad. Somewhere far away where she could never bother you again. Somewhere like South Africa. Please say yes, darling.'

Lying in bed beside her, with her soft, pliant body pressed against him, Mahon was too weak to do anything but agree, although the last thing he wanted to do was to flee to South Africa with her. He made one last attempt to temporize. 'It's all very well speaking of leaving the country, darling. But there's the matter of finding the money for the fares, to say nothing of the problem of supporting ourselves until I get a job.'

'You needn't worry about the fares, or keeping ourselves until you manage to get a job,' Emily said triumphantly. 'I have £600 invested in shares which I could draw out.'

'Have you now?' Mahon said, brightening. He thought about it for a few moments, and then gave her one of his winning smiles. 'I can see there's no denying you.' He added casually, 'You'd better turn in your shares tomorrow, then we can start making arrangements for us to leave the country.'

It is fairly obvious that at this stage Mahon had no intention of murdering Emily, but only of getting his hands on her money. Her nest egg was a tidy sum in those days, but not enough for him to resort to murder. Embezzlement was another matter, and something that Mahon treated almost as a way of life, depending on his wits to get himself out of trouble should it occur. So why did he feel impelled to murder Emily Kaye and dispose of her body in the nauseating way he did? The simple fact of the matter was that Mahon later discovered Emily was pregnant, an unwelcome piece of news for a man in his position. When examining Mahon's motives we have to remember that Emily Kaye's murder took place in 1924, when having an illegitimate child was not as commonplace as it is now. When she eventually broke the news to him he was faced with what must have seemed to him an impossible situation. He had not the slightest intention of fleeing the country with her, which would have meant giving up a well-paid job and deserting his wife and child, a façade of respectability that he had come to value. On the other hand, if he reneged on his promises to her, she would cause a scandal and he would lose his job and become something of a social outcast within the narrow circles in which he moved. To his mind, there was only one answer to the problem. Emily would have to go.

We do not know for certain when Emily told him she was pregnant, but all the evidence produced at the trial proves beyond all doubt that he knew before he met her in Eastbourne on that fateful day in April 1924.

Before then much had happened. Emily had sold her shares and had deposited the money in the bank, then had drawn £400 which she had handed over to Mahon. In what must have seemed to her a touching gesture of good faith he had bought her an expensive ring, which she proudly showed to her room-mate Eileen Warren, who had looked at it with some surprise. She had met Mahon on several occasions, and he had never once given her the impression of being sufficiently in love with Emily to give up a good job and his wife and child for an uncertain future in South Africa. Deciding not to voice her misgivings, she admired the ring and wished her well.

From then on events proceeded rapidly. 'It's all fixed!' he told Emily one day. 'I've a number of business matters to clear up first. Then I'll meet up with you in Eastbourne. From there we'll be going on to Paris, where we'll stay until after the Easter holidays. Then we're going through France and then Italy, from where we'll be sailing to the Cape.' He smiled. 'You'd better get packed right away, dear. I've booked you in at the Kenilworth Hotel from the 7th.'

Overjoyed, Emily rushed back to her room and began packing. Her room-mate was not there, and she resolved to write to her from Eastbourne, apologizing for not seeing her before she left and telling her if she wanted to get in touch, to write care of the Standard Bank in Cape Town.

Arriving at the hotel on 7 April she wrote her letter to Eileen and then waited for Mahon, who arrived in Eastbourne on the 4.45 train on the 10th. Early in the day he had gone shopping and had bought a large cook's knife and a meat saw. When she came down to meet him at the reception desk he greeted her with an engaging smile. 'A slight change of plan, dearest ... As we've plenty of time to catch the sailing, I decided at the last moment to rent a bungalow along the coast where we can really be alone. I hope you have no objections.'

Poor, gullible Emily was only too happy to go along with anything, as long as at the end of it all she landed up in Cape Town with the man she loved. She left the hotel soon afterwards with Mahon, and was never seen again – unless you count the remnants of her which were to turn up some time later.

The bungalow, which Mahon had rented under the name of Waller, lay between Eastbourne and Pevensey Bay in an area known as The Crumbles. It was a lonely and slightly run-down spot which few people chose to visit, and one where Emily Kaye could be murdered with little fear of interruption. Did he have any feelings of guilt while he was taking her to the bungalow? None at all. For by then he had already met someone with whom he was hoping to embark on yet another brief affair.

Her name was Ethel Primrose Duncan, and he had met her on the same day that Emily had travelled down to Eastbourne. It was raining heavily that night when she had the misfortune to encounter Mahon. After making a few comments about the appalling weather he had offered to see her home. 'It's late, and dangerous for a good-looking woman like yourself to be out alone,' he told her, his rather prominent and strong-looking jaw giving him the deceptive look of a reliable man who could be trusted not to misbehave himself.

Instead of sending him on his way with a withering look, Ethel agreed to let him walk her to her home in Isleworth. Before he left her in front of the house which she shared with her sister, she had agreed to see him again. Although she could hardly have known it, she was soon to become the innocent participant in a bizarre and horrifying situation which must have haunted her for the rest of her life.

They met again in London on the 15th, when they dined together. Earlier the same day Mahon had murdered Emily Kaye, whose body now lay in one of the bedrooms, covered with a coat. She was to lie there for another four days before he began the grisly task of dismembering her.

Over dinner on that evening of the 15th, Mahon calmly suggested that Ethel should come over and stay at the bungalow the following weekend. Although she hardly knew him she agreed. It was an unwise decision on her part, to say the least, but an all too understandable one. She was thirty-two, lonely and with little experience of men, and she had been completely captivated by Mahon, whose insouciant charm had swept more worldly women than herself off their feet. He met her at Eastbourne Station the following Friday, dressed in a smart suit and looking totally relaxed, even though only hours before he had been busy dismembering Emily's body and stuffing her remains safely away in a trunk in one of the bungalow's bedrooms.

Did Mahon take a ghoulish delight in setting up this macabre situation? Or was his behaviour the action of a psychopath who was so impervious to all human feelings that he could sleep with someone while the remains of the woman he had just murdered lay in the next bedroom? As the law in those days was not greatly concerned with the mental state of a murderer, we shall never know.

Ethel Duncan shared Mahon's bed from Easter Friday until the following Monday, when they both returned to London. They had dinner and then took in a show that was playing at the London Palladium. Afterwards he put her on a train to Eastbourne, promising to get in touch with her shortly.

When Mahon made his own way home that night he must have felt that he had covered his tracks quite well.

Although murder had not been on the agenda in the beginning, he had been careful to hide his relationship with Emily from his business colleagues, though it had remained a potentially dangerous situation until she had left the company to work elsewhere in the city. The only person who had known of their relationship was Eileen Warren and, as far as she was concerned, the two of them were now on their way to South Africa, a story which Emily had lent credence to with her farewell note to Eileen. As for Ethel Duncan, she had known Mahon as Patrick Waller, the name he had given when he had rented the bungalow.

It was true that two heart-stopping situations had occurred at the bungalow, but he had evaded them easily enough. One arose when Ethel came across a pair of Emily's shoes and some of her toiletries. 'They must have been left by my wife,' he said quickly. 'She was down here recently.'

The other occurred when she discovered him screwing up the door of the bedroom next to where they were sleeping. 'The door doesn't lock properly,' he told her. 'There are some very valuable books in there that belong to a friend of mine. So obviously I have to make the room secure.' Ethel had accepted his explanation without question.

All the same, he could not have slept well that night. He still had to dispose of the body, a gruesome task that even Mahon could not have been relishing.

What followed next is the stuff of nightmares.

The next morning he went down to the bungalow where he spent all day trying to burn the remains in the sitting-room grate. But it is not easy to destroy a body completely by burning it and by nightfall, he had only managed to get rid of the head and the legs. Exhausted, and now in a state of near hysteria, he went home and stayed away from the bungalow until he could steel himself to resume his horrific task. This was not until the Saturday, when Emily

Kaye had already been dead for more than a week.

When he went to the bungalow for the second time he tried boiling down portions of the body to a slurry which he could dispose of down the lavatory. When he could see he was getting nowhere, he then set to work on the body like a demented butcher. When he had finished, all he had to show for his efforts were a number of chunks of mangled flesh, some of which he wrapped up into brown paper parcels and placed in a large Gladstone bag, together with a number of small items and some pieces of Emily's clothing which he had forgotten to burn. When he finally left the bungalow that night, it looked more like a charnel-house than a holiday home.

After getting rid of the parcels by throwing them out of the window of the railway carriage to rot away in the dense undergrowth which lay along much of the track in those days, he was unable to face going home and got off the train at Reading. After spending a sleepless night in a hotel, he went on to Waterloo Station where he deposited the bag in left luggage, intending to pick it up some time before proceeding to Eastbourne to make yet another attempt to deal with what was left of Emily Kaye.

So far little mention has been made of Mrs Mahon. What were her feelings about his continual absences from home? One must remember once again that this occurred in the 1920s when a man was considered master of his own home, with the right to come and go as he pleased. Apart from anything else, he was a sales manager, a position which gave him the ideal excuse for being away, visiting customers. Even so, Mrs Mahon knew her husband well enough to know that something was going on, and for this reason had been going through his pockets for some time, but without success. But on his return from Eastbourne she did find something – a cloakroom ticket.

There was nothing incriminating about this in itself. But Mrs Mahon was puzzled, for some reason which has never been explained. Emily Kaye was killed at a time in the country's social history when interest in murder had become something of a national pastime, with each case given enormous coverage in the national press. Did Mrs Mahon suspect that her husband had joined the long line of killers, whose cases seemed in danger of clogging up the machinery of the law courts? It is possible, but not likely. In all probability she was simply curious to know what her husband had left at Waterloo Station. This is borne out by the fact that she turned to a friend who was the one person who could find the answer to that question without trouble – a former railway detective.

He took the ticket away and returned with it the next day, telling her to replace it. He was grim-faced and did not tell her what he had found after prising open the bag. What he had done, however, was to communicate his findings to the police, who were already at the station, waiting for Mahon to appear.

When Mahon eventually turned up to claim the bag, he was immediately arrested and taken to the Kennington Police Station, where the bag was opened in his presence. Inside were a pair of women's panties and a number of other garments, as well as a ten-inch carving knife and a racquet case engraved with Emily Kaye's initials. All of them were soaked with blood. When asked to explain the blood on the clothing, Mahon said weakly, 'I'm fond of dogs. I must have been carrying meat around for them.'

'As far as we know, you haven't got any dogs,' he was told.

Mahon was silent.

After sitting there for nearly half an hour without saying anything, Mahon told his interrogators the story he was to repeat at his trial.

Today, murder cases do not attract the same attention as they did when Patrick Mahon went on trial for the murder of Emily Kaye. The abolition of capital punishment has removed the one dramatic element in a trial which brought the public flocking in their droves to watch the spectacle of a man fighting for his life against the machinery of the law, more often than not reaching its conclusion with the judge putting on the black cap that was the signal that the accused was about to be sentenced to death by hanging.

Before Mahon went on trial, the press had already had a field day, reporting what the police had found when they had entered the bungalow. The public was spared nothing. Nor did they want their feelings spared. With morbid fascination they read how the police had found the quartered and limbless remains of Emily Kaye lying in a trunk, and how the heart and other organs had been found in a biscuit tin. By the time the press was finished, Mahon had already been judged and found guilty by most of the public.

When he came to trial at the Sussex Assizes in Lewes on 15 July 1924, the public's morbid appetite for the sensational had been whetted to such an extent that the court-house was mobbed, the crowds hoping to get a glimpse of him. If the two hundred who were finally allowed into the court were expecting to see a cringing monster who looked the part, they were to be disappointed. Instead they saw a pleasant-faced and well-dressed man, whose hair was immaculately in place. They settled in their seats and waited expectantly for the trial to begin.

The trial was presided over by Mr Justice Avory, who came in looking like a harbinger of doom with his heavily lined face set in a disapproving look which boded ill for the prisoner. Appearing for the prosecution was Sir Henry Curtis Brown, who was soon to demolish Mahon's feeble defence. Acting on behalf of Mahon was Mr J.D. Cassels, who must have been well aware of the impossible task which lay ahead of him, though none of this showed in his face as he sat there, riffling through the enormous stack of notes that lay in front of him.

When Sir Henry rose to his feet that day he began quietly, but as he got into his stride, almost every sentence he uttered was a lethal blow designed to destroy the defence before it had even started. He began by reading two statements that Mahon had made at the police station. When he had finished he looked up at the jury. 'As you have just heard,' he said, 'the defence of the prisoner is that this case is not one of murder, but of death by misadventure. It is the case for the Crown that it was no such thing, as you will be able to judge for yourself when you have heard all the evidence.'

Death by misadventure? This was indeed Mahon's defence, and possibly the only one he had thought might just get him off. But if there had been the slightest chance of him getting away with that plea, he had already scuppered himself by being in possession of the knife and meat saw, which he had bought *before* he went down to meet Emily Kaye at Eastbourne. Once the prosecution had established this, Mahon's defence was in shreds.

But even before that, the jury must have already made up its mind that Mahon was guilty as charged. On the third day of the trial Miss Ethel Duncan took the stand. Faced with Mahon again she burst into tears, before giving her evidence in an almost inaudible voice. It was enough in itself to brand him a cold and callous murderer who had been capable of sleeping with her while the dismembered corpse of Emily Kaye had lain in the next room. By the time she had finished, Mahon's neck was already in the hangman's noose. All that Sir Henry had to do now was to tighten it.

Mr Cassels did his best for his client. He put Mahon on the stand, where he began a long, rambling story of how Miss Kaye had kept pressurizing him to leave his wife, until he had reluctantly agreed to take her on a fortnight's holiday, when she would convince him he would be happy with her by a passionate display of lovemaking.

The 'love experiment', as Mahon had called it, had ended in tragedy when they had quarrelled and Miss Kaye had attacked him with an axe. He was grappling with her for possession of the weapon when she had fallen and struck her head on an iron cauldron that stood in the fireplace.

'She was dead within seconds,' Mahon said, his voice thick with emotion. 'Knowing that I would be accused of murder, I panicked and decided the only course open to me was to dispose of the body.'

Mahon wept when he told the court how he had dismembered the body. None of it made any difference. Neither Mr Cassels' valiant attempts to save him nor his own attempts to arouse sympathy made the slightest difference to the outcome of the trial. Not only had the jury now heard Miss Duncan's evidence, but they had also heard the country's foremost forensic pathologist, Sir Bernard Spilsbury, who had stated that Emily Kaye had been pregnant when she was murdered, and, though he was not able to establish how Mahon had actually murdered her, that it was impossible for her to have received a fatal injury from the cauldron. They had also heard the evidence of Miss Eileen Warren, who had sketched in Mahon's early relationship with Miss Kaye, and revealed it to be one based on lies and deceit. Most telling of all had been Mahon's purchase of the knife and meat saw.

The final speeches were little more than a formality. Mr Justice Avory's summing up lasted an hour and a half, and the jury then went out. They returned in less than forty minutes with their verdict – guilty.

Before being sentenced to death, Mahon launched into an unexpected tirade in which he denounced 'the bitterness and unfairness' of the summing up. When he left the court he looked genuinely aggrieved.

Mahon was executed in Wandsworth Prison less than two months later. Although our English courts have seen the occasional miscarriage of justice, this was not one of them.

THE CUPBOARD LOVER

Otto Sanhuber and Walburga Oesterreich

American murder case 1922

The three main players in this bizarre story were an unlikeable trio. There was Fred Oesterreich, an arrogant and brutish-faced German who was detested by the entire staff of his factory, which he owned and ran like some demented Prussian officer, roaming the factory floor barking orders and chivvying his staff to greater efforts until they could have cheerfully murdered him, given the chance. He was a bully and a tyrant.

Then there was his wife Walburga, who was of German stock, tinged with Spanish blood. A formidable-looking woman of robust proportions, she more than equalled her husband when it came to a shouting match, which occurred frequently in the Oesterreich household. She was also a nymphomaniac.

Finally, there was Otto Sanhuber, an undersized youth of seventeen, with a receding chin and watery blue eyes that looked out apprehensively at the world through a pair of silver-rimmed glasses. He was the very last person you could imagine as being a sex object, keeping a woman like Walburga happy for more than nineteen years.

It all began in Milwaukee, Wisconsin, in the United States, in 1903. Fred and Walburga had been married for fifteen years, and they were not happy together. From Walburga's point of view, the one who was at fault was her husband. Although he had nearly a quarter of a million dollars stashed away in the bank, he had suddenly become extremely mean with his money. They were also childless, something for which she blamed her husband – and not without some cause. He had been drinking heavily for

several years, thereby lowering his sexual prowess to such
a degree that it was now virtually non-existent. Walburga
could put up with his meanness and his boorish behaviour,
but the one thing she could not abide in a man was an
inability to perform in bed. Now she was saddled with
such a man it was an intolerable situation for someone of
her proclivity. In her frustration she began to throw the
china around. A brutal overseer in his own factory, Fred
could only cower in a corner while the crockery rained
around him. Such was Walburga's fury, that she could
have ended up by killing Fred with a well-aimed blow
with a flat iron. Fortunately, help was at hand.

Walburga spent part of the day at the factory, where she
tried to undo the damage that Fred had done. Unlike
Fred, she realized that if you wish to keep good staff you
had to treat them well. She was fighting a losing battle, but
at least the staff did not detest her. It was during one of
her regular visits to the factory that one of the sewing
machines broke down. A repair man was summoned, and
in due course Otto Sanhuber arrived on the scene.

As soon as she saw Otto, Walburga knew that he was
the answer to all her problems. What she saw in him was a
mystery. As well as looking like one of nature's rejects, he
was painfully shy and looked too undernourished to carry
out the gruelling work that Walburga had in store for him.
For all that, she just *knew* that he was the right young man
for her.

After that, Walburga saw to it that Otto was often
called out to deal with one of the sewing machines which,
inexplicably, were now always going wrong. Their relationship developed until she decided that the time was
ripe and she asked him over to deal with yet another
sewing machine problem – but this time at her house.
Dressed in a dressing gown and drenched in a heady
perfume, she met him on the doorstep.

'The machine is in the upper bedroom,' she told him.
'I'd better show you where it is.'

Otto dutifully followed her up to the bedroom, where Walburga lay on the bed while Otto proceeded to repair the machine. When he had finished, she called over to him. 'Do come over here,' she cooed.

Until then Otto had not so much as laid a finger on a woman. No girl would have allowed it, except out of pity, a commodity that was in short supply in Milwaukee where most single girls were too busy trying to find themselves a husband to be kind to lame ducks. Walburga was not bothered with the minor details of Otto looking such a sorry example of young manhood. As he moved to her bedside, she pulled him roughly towards her and folded her arms around him in a nutcracker-like embrace.

When Otto left the house that late autumn afternoon, it was with the knowledge that he was now a man. If he did not actually skip home, he was certainly in a buoyant mood. Walburga had not found him wanting in the area which she cared for most, and there were more such afternoons to come, she had promised him.

This happy state of affairs for both of them lasted for three years, with Otto scuttling into the house whenever the opportunity presented itself, which Walburga made certain was regularly.

Then one day Fred Oesterreich came back to the house and confronted his wife with some disturbing news. 'You've been seeing another man,' he accused her. 'I've been informed by an anonymous person that they've seen a man regularly entering the house and staying for a long time before he leaves.'

'Rubbish!' Walburga said succinctly. 'People like to make trouble, just for the sake of it.'

Fred Oesterreich let it go at that. His wife had been surprisingly placid for the last three years, and he had no wish to start making trouble at home for no good reason.

Although Walburga had managed to lull her husband's suspicions, she was worried. Otto had more than fulfilled her expectations of him, but she had no wish to lose her husband, who was a rich man and stood every chance of dying before she did, at which time she would become a rich widow who could do as she liked. Until that happy day came she had to be careful. To begin with, Otto's regular calls to the house would have to stop. How then could she continue to see him without risking losing Fred for ever?

In desperation she came up with an answer that would need a great deal of courage, both on her part and Otto's – especially as she knew that her husband could become very violent if he ever found out that he was being cuckolded, and in his own home too.

Her plan was breathtaking in its audacity. She would move Otto into the house, where he would live without her husband even knowing it. Understandably, Otto was less than enthusiastic about the idea.

'Don't worry. It's going to be all right,' she assured him. 'Wait until you've seen the hiding place I've chosen for you.'

We now come to the most incredible aspect of this case. While Fred Oesterreich was away one day, making his staff's lives a misery in the factory, Otto was smuggled into the house and taken up to the attic, which was reached through a trap-door above the master bedroom.

'This is where you'll stay,' Walburga announced.

'It's very small,' Otto said dubiously. 'It's little better than a cupboard.'

'I'll make it comfortable,' Walburga said. 'I'll get a single bed up here and then furnish it with a table, a rug and a couple of chairs. It'll be just like home.'

A home it wasn't, but Otto eventually fell in with Walburga's scheme. Despite his unprepossessing exterior, in him lurked the spirit of a romantic and daring adventurer, qualities that were to add an unexpected twist to this strange story. Also he had become extremely fond of Walburga, who had made him feel wanted for the first time in his life. An orphan who had had a hard upbringing, he had seen little joy until he had met her. She had transformed everything; it was little wonder that he was prepared to risk everything so that they could stay together.

Before he took up residence in the attic, some strict house rules had to be observed, Walburga told him. He was to keep silent and not to move around when Fred was in the house. She would put a lock on Otto's side of the trap-door to prevent her husband from trying to get in. If he tried, and failed to get in, he would assume that the trap-door had jammed.

Otto would be allowed to come out during the day to exercise or to have sex with Walburga. Otherwise he would stay quietly in the attic until he received three raps on the trap-door, which would be the signal that it was all right to come down. He would be allowed candles, but he was to keep away from the small window as there was always the danger that some prying neighbour might see him. Walburga would supply him with food regularly. 'We must feed you up,' she said fondly. 'You need a little more flesh on you.'

It was true. Although time had gone by, Otto had not filled out, and he was still as undersized as he had been when she had first met him. For this we probably have to blame Walburga for her continual demands on Otto, who was still a growing lad.

Once he had settled in, Otto decided that his new abode was ideal for a person of his simple tastes. He was fed like a fighting cock by Walburga who saw to it that he had nothing but the best, though his diet was a particularly German one, consisting mostly of various forms of sausage and cheese, washed down with milk. Fred Oester-reich's housekeeping bill must have risen alarmingly, but he said nothing. When Otto was not downstairs taking his daily exercise, or looking after Walburga's needs, he passed the time reading the adventure stories that she brought him from the library. It must have been a

claustrophobic sort of life, but it didn't seem to worry
Otto in the slightest.

Two years passed in this manner without Fred having
an inkling of what was going on under his own roof. It was
true that there had been a few nasty moments, one of
them being when Fred had discovered food missing from
the fridge, and another when he had sat bolt upright in
bed and complained of hearing sounds of movement
above his head. Then he had noticed that someone had
been at his cigars. Otto had taken up smoking.

'It may have escaped your notice, but I don't happen to
smoke cigars,' Walburga had said tartly. 'You drink too
much and now your mind is beginning to give way. I think
you should see a doctor.'

Now a worried man, Fred went to see the local doctor,
who wrote out a prescription and told him to give up
drinking. For a long time afterwards the bully of the shop
floor was a subdued man.

In the meantime, Otto had found his *métier* in life.
After waking up one morning, he had suddenly felt the
urge to become a writer. Having been living on a diet of
pulp fiction for the last two years, his literary sights were
not aimed high. Even so, the rejection slips came back
with monotonous regularity to the post office box which
Walburga had rented for him under an assumed name.

The days went by and Otto kept churning out his
adventure stories, until suddenly he began to sell. From
then on there was no stopping him. Stories began to pour
from his pen, and as he wrote them Walburga typed them
and sent them off to the publishers. They may not have
been the kind of stories that receive the attention of
serious writers, but most of them sold and brought Otto a
useful income of his own.

In 1913, ten years after Otto had met Walburga Oesterreich, her husband decided the time had come for them to
move house. Walburga tried to dissuade him, but he was
adamant. They were going to move, he told her. His

health had deteriorated suddenly, and the doctor had told him that a move would be beneficial.

Instead of accepting the situation and sadly sending Otto on his way, Walburga decided that he would move with them. One can but only admire her dogged determination to keep a good thing going.

Time had marched on for all of them. Otto was now twenty-seven and Walburga Oesterreich forty-seven. As for poor Fred Oesterreich, the years had dealt harshly with him and he was still hearing things. Otto was becoming careless. When they finally moved, Otto presumably went into lodgings until the Oesterreichs got straight and Walburga was ready to receive him. As he had not ventured once outside the house in all the time he had lived there, he must have found the outside world strange.

Once they had all settled in their new home, everyone carried on in much the same way as they had done before. Fred continued to drink too much, and Walburga continued to have Otto in her bed with unfailing regularity. As for Otto, he was just grateful to be home again with Walburga, who had been careful to guide her husband in the direction of a house which had suitable accommodation for Otto.

Mrs Oesterreich and her lover were happy to continue in this familiar pattern indefinitely. Each morning, Fred went off early to his factory, and as soon as he was gone Otto came down to have breakfast and then went back to his writing until he heard a peremptory knock on the trapdoor, telling him that Walburga wanted him. Soon Otto's memories of his brief and unwelcome sojourn in the outside world became a distant memory, not to be repeated.

But the halcyon days of Otto Sanhuber were gradually drawing to a close. When Fred Oesterreich unexpectedly came back drunk early one evening, his arrival home coincided with one of Otto's raids on the fridge. Not remembering him after all those years, and thinking him an intruder, Fred threw him out of the house before reeling up to the bedroom, where Walburga was sitting up in bed looking as pale as death. After telling her what had happened, he then fell into bed, leaving Walburga wondering how her poor Otto was faring, shut out of his own home. While Fred lay in a drunken stupor beside her, she had time to marshal her thoughts. Once more she was equal to the occasion.

'I've been thinking, Fred,' she said to her husband the next morning. 'I think we should sell up and move to California.' She gave him a look of tender concern, something she seldom bestowed on Fred. 'You're not in the best of health and the sun will do you good.'

Fred needed some persuading, and one can understand why. At the time, Milwaukee was considered to have one of the most healthy climates in the United States, and he had many kindred spirits there, as half the population was either German or of German extraction. His business was thriving and he had become set in a way of life he liked. But the city had grown enormously since he had first settled there, and factories were springing up all over the place, creating competition where none had existed before. Perhaps going to California was not such a bad idea after all, Fred finally decided. The pace was slower there, and he could buy another premises more cheaply while making an enormous profit on his present building. Before he left for the factory, he had agreed they should go to California.

Otto sneaked back into the house as soon as he had gone, and Walburga told him what was happening. 'You're getting too careless, and it's not safe for you to stay here any more,' she said. Seeing the expression of dismay on Otto's face, she added, 'Don't worry. I've persuaded Fred we'd be better off in California. Now this is what we'll do ...'

Otto was to go to California and get himself a job, and

Walburga would keep in touch with him by means of a post office box. When the Oesterreichs moved to California, he would then be able to move in with them again. 'It won't be long before you're with me again,' she assured him.

It took two years before Fred Oesterreich was able to get the price he wanted for his factory and they were able to sell up and move to Los Angeles. In the meantime, Otto had got himself a job as a porter in an apartment block.

In 1918 the Oesterreichs arrived in Los Angeles, where Fred bought a large residence which his wife had been careful to vet before she allowed her husband to sign on the dotted line. Once she had seen that it had a suitable attic room for Otto, she told him that she thought it would do very nicely. Within a few days of moving in, Otto was once more part of the family household.

Four more years passed. In that time Fred had bought himself into a business, and Otto and Walburga had long since settled back into their old cosy relationship. Then on 22 August 1922, the neighbours heard a series of revolver shots. The police were summoned, and when they entered the house, it was to discover Fred Oesterreich lying on the floor riddled with bullets, and Walburga screaming for help in one of the upstairs rooms. When they found her, locked in a cupboard, she gave a bravura performance in which hysteria, horror and shock at Fred's sudden and unexpected demise were nicely blended. Between sobs she told them how she had returned with her husband that evening to find themselves confronted with an armed burglar. Poor, fearless Fred had tried to tackle the burglar, who had cold-bloodedly shot him in his tracks. He had then bundled her upstairs and locked her in the closet before making his getaway. Later, when the distraught widow had composed herself sufficiently to answer questions, she was asked if the burglar had taken anything.

'I don't think he had time to steal much,' she told the

police. 'That is, except for the diamond-studded timepiece
he took from my poor husband before he pushed me in
the closet.'

The police were not satisfied with her story, but they
could prove nothing except that she had a motive – that of
financial gain in the event of her husband's death. As this
hardly constituted evidence in itself, they were forced to
release her.

What had really happened on that fateful night was that
the Oesterreichs had returned home in the evening and, as
soon as they were in the house, had begun quarrelling
violently. Hearing the uproar going on downstairs, Otto
had become so alarmed that he had gone to where he
knew Walburga kept a .25 revolver. Armed with it he had
then raced downstairs and confronted Fred. Instead of
backing away, Fred had come at him, and in a blind panic
Otto had fired at him several times before Fred had fallen
dead at his feet.

Otto was a simpleton in many ways, but not when it
came to concocting a plot, as long as it was a fairly basic
one. Removing Fred's timepiece from his body, he handed
it to Walburga, telling her to hide it somewhere before
shutting her in the closet and locking it. Afterwards, he
had retired to his attic room, leaving Walburga to deal
with the police.

Many years were to pass before all this came out at the
trial. Again, a great deal had happened in the intervening
years. Fred Oesterreich's business affairs were found to be
in a complete muddle, and his widow had been forced to
call in a lawyer named Herman Shipiro, who had sorted
out the legal tangle so well that Walburga had been
prompted to give him her late husband's diamond-
studded watch. That was her first mistake. There were
others. After starting an affair with Shipiro she then told
him about Otto and got him to connive in Otto's escape to
Vancouver.

Shipiro then realized that he had placed himself in a

dangerous position. By helping Walburga and being a party to everything that had gone on, he now represented the only person who could be a danger to her. Knowing that she was a headstrong woman, capable of taking the most appalling chances, his nerve broke and he went to the police. After telling them that he was in fear of his life, to 'clear his conscience' he made an affidavit regarding the death of Fred Oesterreich. As a result, Walburga and Otto were both charged with murder.

They were charged separately, and Otto was the first to face a judge and jury. He was now married, but he had not prospered since he had been away from Walburga's loving care and attention. It showed in every line of his defeated-looking face, and the jury could only stare at him in wonder as the incredible story of the long-standing affair was unfolded before the court on a hot summer's day in 1930. His pathetic air of a man who was unable to cope with life was enough in itself to make the jury believe his story that he had fired the bullets into Fred Oesterreich in a blind frenzy of fear, rather than as an act of calculated murder. They brought in a verdict of manslaughter, knowing there was a three-year statute of limitations for the crime of manslaughter. As Fred Oesterreich had been killed long before that period, Otto was allowed to walk out of the court a free man. He disappeared from sight soon afterwards and was never heard of again.

Now it was the turn of Walburga Oesterreich. She came to court with the best defence lawyer that money could buy. This was Jerry Giesler, an already famous Hollywood defence lawyer who was to make an even greater reputation for himself defending some of Hollywood's famous stars, including Errol Flynn, successfully represented years later in a rape charge.

It was Giesler's contention that his client was guilty of nothing more than not coming forward at the right time. When Walburga took the stand she was sixty-three. If she had ever been in love with Otto, it soon became clear that love had now flown out of the window. She blamed him for everything, painting him as a mini monster who had lived off her for years, and had turned her craving for sex to his own advantage. When he had shot her husband she had kept quiet rather than have to face the embarrassment of her love life being made public.

The jury couldn't come to an agreement about her part in her husband's death, and they were dismissed. Incredibly, her case hung fire until 1936, when the District Attorney finally gave up in despair and had the case against Walburga dropped.

Although both Otto and Walburga got away with it, with nothing more than a great deal of unwelcome publicity, Walburga Oesterreich did not enjoy a comfortable old age. She invested unwisely in the Stock Market, and lost nearly all her money. She was last heard of in the early forties, when she was living in rooms above a garage, before she moved on and was also never heard of again.

THE PYJAMA GIRL

Tony Agostini

Australian murder case 1934

The case of the Pyjama Girl, as she became known to the press, was first brought to the attention of the public in September 1934. On the first day of that month a woman's body was discovered in a culvert a few miles outside Albury, New South Wales. She was dressed in a pair of yellow crêpe oriental-style pyjamas, decorated with a green dragon motif. The thighs and buttocks had been exposed and the head covered with a badly scorched sack. When this was removed it revealed that a white towel edged with blue and red was wrapped around the head, which had been smashed in with a heavy, blunt instrument. Apart from being bludgeoned, she had also been shot in the side of the head.

The first reaction of many people to the news was that the murder had been committed by some Aborigine, who had been so inflamed by the sight of a white woman in her pyjamas that he had raped and murdered her. There was no logical reason for this assumption, which was based on nothing more than a blind hatred for the Aborigines, which seems to have been shared by almost everyone, with the exception of the more enlightened settlers, who were few and far between in those days.

This climate of hatred and contempt which extended to all coloured people had been fostered by the government's determination to create a 'white Australia', in which the Aborigines, Chinese, Papuans and Japanese were there only to provide cheap labour. At the bottom of the pile were the Aborigines, considered little better than vermin by the ordinary man and woman in the street, who were

fond of quoting the immortal words of a member of the
West Australian Parliament: 'It will be a happy day for
Australia when the natives and kangaroos disappear.'

Fortunately, Inspector Goodsell, who was summoned to
the scene of the murder, had a more open mind than
most.

After examining the body, which was that of a blonde-
haired and not unattractive woman in her mid-twenties,
he got to his feet and looked around him. The first thing
he saw were some skid marks which looked as if they had
been made by a motor car. If he had suspected at all that
the murder had been committed by an Aborigine, he now
dismissed that possibility on two counts. Normally, Aborigines did not own pistols, and neither did they drive cars,
let alone own them.

Inspector Goodsell knew instinctively that this was not
going to be an easy case. Before they could proceed with
the investigation, the identity of the dead woman had to
be established. This would take time, but it was not an
insurmountable problem. There was, after all, the towel,
the sack and the pyjamas, which should all yield something eventually. There was also the bullet, still to be
extracted from the skull of the dead woman, and her
teeth. Once plaster casts had been made and photographs
of them circulated to all the dentists in the country, it
could only be a matter of elimination before the identity
of the dead woman was established.

When the body was finally taken to the mortuary,
Inspector Goodsell was in a reasonably optimistic mood.
With a little luck, the case could be closed and the
murderer brought to justice within a matter of months.
But this was to be very far from the truth. The file on the
case was not closed until 1944 – ten years after the body
had been found.

By the time the case was solved, more by chance than
anything else, the case of the Pyjama Girl had become one
of the most famous crimes in the annals of Australian

police history. To understand how the Pyjama Girl came
to be on exhibition to the public for most of that time, we
must go back to when the police were brought to a dead
halt with their investigations.

Photographs of the towel and the sack had been circulated all over the country, before the police learned that
both items had been mass-produced and therefore could
not be traced to any individual. No dentist had any
records that could match the photograph and description
of the dead woman's teeth, and they had been equally
unlucky with the bullet they had taken out of the dead
woman's skull. This had proved to be a .25 bullet fired
from a Webley Scott automatic. Everyone who owned
such a pistol had been approached and their guns checked
against the bullet. But there again they had drawn a blank.
It was as if the Pyjama Girl had never existed.

In desperation, the police decided on a macabre course
of action which had never been taken before and was to
make this case so famous in Australia. They would put the
body on public display in the hope that someone would
come along who would be able to identify the corpse. A
zinc-lined bath was made and then taken to Sydney
University where it was filled with formalin to preserve the
body once it had been lowered into the bath. To
encourage the public to come and view the body, two
rewards were offered, one for information leading to the
body being identified, and another more substantial one
for information leading to the apprehension and conviction of the murderer. For the first few weeks the public
came in such large numbers that the queues outside the
university resembled those outside a cinema showing the
latest movie from America. But not one single person
gave the police information of any value.

The police had all but given up hope of getting the body
identified when they had a stroke of luck which was far
greater than they realized at the time. Years later they
were to reproach themselves for not seeing that they had

been on the verge of solving the case. The less charitable
could say, with some truth, that they had allowed the
murderer to slip through their fingers through sheer
laziness.

When the body had first been examined in the
mortuary, it was noticed that the ears were oddly
misshapen with lobes so small as to be almost non-
existent. This information had been published in the
newspapers but there had been no immediate reaction to
it.

Then suddenly the police had some news that was to
galvanize them into action. At last someone had come
forward to tell them that they had known a woman with
malformed ears such as those described in the press. Her
name had been Linda Platt, who had emigrated from
England in 1927, and had worked for some time as an
usherette at the Strand Theatre in Sydney, where she had
met and later married an Italian named Tony Agostini.

All this proved to be true. Linda and her husband had
lived in the King's Cross area, where they had resided in
Kellett Street for several years before suddenly disappearing from the scene, leaving no forwarding address.

The question now was – where had they moved to after
they had left Sydney? Apart from the big cities, there were
countless small townships, most of them with inadequate
records of their residents. To complicate matters further,
Australia was a country of transients moving from one
place to another in their restless search for some sort of
security in a land which was still in the throes of a depression that had been going on since the 1920s. In all it took
ten months before they were able to track them down to
an address in Melbourne – and even then the case was
only halfway to being solved.

'Linda left me a year ago,' Tony Agostini told the two
detectives who had come knocking at his door in Swanston Street.

'Any idea where she is now?' he was asked.

Tony shrugged. 'Who knows? The last I heard of her she was working as a hairdresser for the Union Steamship Line.'

One of the detectives produced a photograph. 'Is this her?'

To their surprise, Tony shook his head. 'No – that's not her.' He looked at the photograph again and then turned away. 'She was a lush,' he said bitterly. 'I did my best, but it was no good. In the end she went out one day and never came back.'

The two detectives left it at that. Before departing they asked him to call in at the police station in Russell Street the following morning, just in case there were more questions they wanted to ask.

It is at this point that the behaviour of the police seems quite baffling to the outsider. When Agostini reported to the police station the following morning he was left waiting for several hours, before he finally left, without seeing anyone. He called again twice, and each time his name was taken at the desk, but still no one bothered to come and see him. When he left after his third visit, he did not bother to return. What is even more inexplicable is that they do not seem to have bothered to show the photograph of the Pyjama Girl to any of Linda's neighbours or acquaintances. If they had, much time and public money would have been saved and they would have closed a case which was to drag on for another eight years.

Whatever glimmer of interest that might have remained over the identity of the dead woman was extinguished with the advent of the Second World War. The body's removal to Police Headquarters therefore passed almost unnoticed, as did Tony Agostini's banishment to an internment camp after he had been unwise enough to start writing pro-Mussolini articles for the local newspapers. He stayed there until 1944, when he was released for some obscure reason known only to the authorities.

It was not the best of times for an enemy alien to find

work, but Tony remembered that he had some old friends
in Sydney where he had worked for some time as a waiter.
Perhaps they could pull a few strings and get him his old
job back? They could and did, and in no time at all Tony
Agostini was back at Romano's, a restaurant whose clien-
tele was always more interested in what was on the plate
before them than who had served it. He could therefore
have stayed there for years, scurrying from table to table
and collecting his tips without ever being recognized by
someone likely to ask awkward questions. But as luck
would have it, Tony was eventually recognized – and by
the one person who was capable of unearthing some
skeletons which Tony dearly wished to remain buried.
This was the New South Wales Police Commissioner
William John Mackay, who had been in charge of the case
of the Pyjama Girl since 1935. Seeing him breeze into the
restaurant one lunch time, Tony's heart must have sunk as
Mackay had eaten there regularly when Tony worked
there before.

Although Mackay hadn't seen Tony for years, he
recognized him immediately from the old days. He
threaded his way among the tables, heading in Tony's
direction.

'Hi, Tony. Nice to see you again after all this time.' He
planted himself squarely in front of Tony. 'You remember
me, don't you?'

Tony hesitated for a second, and then nodded. 'Sure.'

Mackay looked at him appraisingly. 'Your wife, did she
ever come back to you?' Seeing the startled look on
Tony's face, he added, 'I was looking at the files on the
case of the Pyjama Girl only the other day, and I see there
was a time when we thought she might have been your
wife. But I guess we were wrong about that.'

'That's right,' Tony said. By now he had recovered
himself. 'No, my wife never came back.'

Mackay nodded and went back to his table. Seeing
Tony again had revived his interest in the forgotten case.

When he went back to his office that afternoon he studied the file for some time and then called in two of his detective sergeants. 'I'm reviving the case of the Pyjama Girl,' he said. He pushed the file across the desk. 'Take this away and study it. Neither of you has been on this case before, so maybe a couple of fresh minds will come up with something.'

After the two detectives had looked at the file, one of the first things they did was go to Melbourne. This time the photograph of the Pyjama Girl was shown to everyone they could find who had known Linda Agostini. To their surprise, a number of people were certain that Linda was the Pyjama Girl.

When this information was brought to Mackay, he nodded. 'It seems that Tony Agostini could be our man.'

'Do you want us to pull him in?' one of the detectives asked.

'Not yet,' Mackay said. 'First, we'll get all those people in Melbourne who knew Linda to look at the body – but not until we've done some work on it. The poor lady is looking rather the worse for wear these days.' He glanced at his calendar. 'Let's set a date for the showing now. Make it 4 March. And while you're about it, get as many people who knew Linda in Sydney as you can. It shouldn't be too difficult.'

Bill Mackay had been right about the Pyjama Girl. Despite the preservative effects of the formalin, the flesh on the face had become soggy and in some parts it had fallen in, giving it an almost skull-like appearance. Mackay set about rectifying this as far as possible. First the body was removed from the bath and dried out and then a woman police officer was called in to try and repair the damage. She did an excellent job. The face had been filled out with wax where necessary and then skilfully made up and treated in such a way as to make it look like living tissue. 'Good,' said Mackay. 'Now let's get in a top hairdresser.'

By the time everyone had finished their work, the features of the dead woman bore more than a reasonable resemblance to those that Detective Inspector Goodsell had seen all those years ago when the body had first been discovered.

On 4 March sixteen people arrived at the Police Headquarters in Sydney, where they were shown the body of the Pyjama Girl. Seven of them immediately recognized her as Linda Agostini.

Tony Agostini was summoned to Mackay's office the same afternoon, when he too was shown the body. 'Still don't recognize her, Tony?' Mackay asked. When Tony shook his head, he commented. 'That's strange. I had sixteen people in here this morning. Nearly half of them identified her as Linda.'

He led the way back to his office where he sat back in his chair and studied Tony, who looked away under the policeman's gaze. 'What's the matter, Tony? You don't look too happy. Perhaps there's something you want to tell me?'

At that point, Tony Agostini broke down and admitted to killing Linda. 'But it was an accident,' he added quickly.

'I think you had better tell me all about it,' Mackay said gently. Like all experienced police officers, he knew a sympathetic approach was best when a suspect was on the verge of making a full confession. He reached for a pen and pad. 'Take your time, Tony.'

Haltingly, Tony began to tell his story, which was one of a man who had been driven to the edge of insanity by his wife's regular drinking bouts which had transformed her into a jealous and vengeful virago. 'She had no cause,' Tony told him. 'I loved that woman. But nothing I could do or say when she was drunk made any difference. To her I was just a lecherous brute who had ruined her life.'

It all came to a head one morning when he woke up to find Linda standing over him with a pistol in her hand. Leaping up, he had struggled for possession of the pistol when it had suddenly gone off and Linda had slumped dead on to the bed.

'One moment she was alive,' Tony said in a low voice. 'The next moment she was dead.'

Numbed by the horror of it all, he had spent hours wandering aimlessly around the house while he tried to work out what he should do. His first option was to go to the police, but more likely than not they would think he had shot Linda during one of the unholy rows which the neighbours had come to accept as a way of life with the Agostinis. Even if he were able to persuade the police it had been an accident, and he managed to get away with a charge of manslaughter, his name would be splashed across the newspapers and from then on he would have been looked down on by the rest of the Italian community, whose own position in Australia had only been won by working hard and keeping themselves out of trouble.

By nightfall Tony had finally come to a decision. He would dispose of the body in some distant and deserted spot before returning home to rebuild his life. As for explaining Linda's absence from the scene, their terrible rows had been something of a talking-point with their neighbours and acquaintances, who would accept without question that she had suddenly left him without a word.

According to Agostini, the rest of the story had been a nightmare which would haunt him for the rest of his life. After dumping the body in the boot of his car, he had driven through the night until he had come to a deserted spot a few miles outside Albury, where he had rolled the body into a culvert. He had then covered the head with a sack, before setting it alight with petrol from his spare can, hoping that the blaze would destroy Linda's features beyond all recognition. On the way back home it had rained heavily, and he had begun to wonder if the blaze had stayed alight under the downpour.

'It didn't,' Mackay said briefly. 'Is there anything else you would like to tell me, Tony?'

'Only that I'm glad it is all over after all this time.'

'I'm sure you are,' Mackay said politely. He did not add that as far as Tony was concerned, it was still very far from being over. Instead, he asked casually, 'What did you do with the gun, Tony?'

'I stopped on the way home and threw it in the river Yarra.'

Mackay sighed. According to the police files, Tony had never owned a gun. Like so many other aspects of the case, vital evidence had either been withheld or had not been on file. More was to come.

'There is one thing more I should mention,' Tony said hesitantly. 'Soon afterwards I told the story to Mr Castellano, a neighbour and friend of mine. I wanted to go to the police then but he advised me against it as he said my story would not be believed.'

'We shall be speaking to your Mr Castellano,' Mackay said grimly. He consulted the notes he had written down. 'This case comes under the jurisdiction of the Melbourne police, Tony. I shall be sending you there tomorrow, accompanied by two detectives.'

After spending the night in the Sydney Police Headquarters, Tony Agostini was taken the next morning to Melbourne, where he was handed over to Inspector Davis. After grilling Tony for several hours, he expressed his dissatisfaction with Tony's answers and charged him with the murder of his wife.

The trial began on 19 July 1944, with Mr Justice Lowe presiding and Mr Casson appearing for the Crown. Acting for the defence was Mr Fazio, who had a more formidable task ahead of him than he had perhaps first realized.

On the surface of it, the case was a straightforward one, and hinged on one thing. Was Agostini's story of how Linda died a true account of the facts? Or had his statement been a complete fabrication built around the one solid piece of evidence that might win him the jury's sympathy – that of Linda's drunken bouts which had led to all those ferocious rows. Even then it seemed that the best verdict Tony could hope for was one of manslaughter. The prosecution, however, was after a verdict of murder, based on the premise that Agostini had become so enraged during one of their rows that he had bludgeoned her to death and then for good measure put a bullet through her head.

'Tell me about your wife's alcoholism,' Mr Casson said, with deceptive mildness, after Tony had taken the stand.

Tony was only too willing to oblige. Relaxed and at ease in the dock, he told the court of all the rows and the accusations that had been hurled at him whenever Linda was drunk. Encouraged by Mr Casson's sympathetic nods, he elaborated on Linda's impossible behaviour which had begun soon after his discovery of empty whisky bottles hidden around the house.

'It must have been enough to make a man want to murder her,' Mr Casson said quietly.

Too late, Tony realized that Mr Casson was skilfully weaving a web around him which would be difficult to escape. But Mr Casson had not finished yet.

'You say in your statement that your wife shot herself in the head while struggling with you?'

'Yes.'

'And what of the other injuries to her head?' Mr Casson asked.

'I also explained those in my statement,' Tony said. 'I was carrying my wife's body downstairs when I slipped and had to let go of her to catch my balance. Linda fell to the bottom of the stairs on to a flower pot which smashed under her weight. When I saw she had cut her head badly on some of the pieces, I wrapped it in a towel to stop the bleeding.'

'Then how is it that the police surgeon who first examined the body was of the opinion that it was not the bullet that killed her, but the multiple injuries inflicted on her skull?'

'That is not possible.'

'It was an opinion shared by other doctors who also examined the body,' Mr Casson said quietly, going in for the kill.

Although the weakest part of Tony's defence was the business of Linda receiving the injuries to the head *after* she had been shot, the jury nevertheless brought in a verdict of 'not guilty of murder, but guilty of manslaughter'. Before passing sentence Mr Justice Lowe had this to say: 'Whatever weapon you used to strike down your wife, it must have been a heavy one and used with great violence ...' He then sentenced Agostini to six years imprisonment with hard labour.

Tony Agostini served nearly four years of his sentence. When he was released, it was to find himself facing a deportation order which was enforced in 1948, when he was placed aboard the *Strathnaver* and sent back to Italy. He was never heard of again.

As for poor Linda, she was finally laid to rest in Melbourne's Preston Cemetery in August 1948, where she still lies, unmourned by anyone, but at least finally free of being a peepshow for the curious.

A SHIPBOARD ROMANCE

James Camb

Murder at sea 1948

There is something about a sea voyage that turns many people's minds to thoughts of having a shipboard romance. Perhaps it is the bracing air and the general feeling of well-being that comes from cutting yourself off from the world and its attendant stresses. Or maybe it is sheer boredom, after having had a surfeit of all those tiresome ship's games that are organized for the benefit of the passengers. Whatever the reason, a shipboard romance is a popular pastime for single men and women, who are either looking for an eligible partner or merely seeking a pleasant dalliance to while away the hours. Not for nothing have our romantic novelists churned out so many books in which a shipboard romance is the starting-point of the plot.

It is an undeniable fact that most young ship's officers see this as one of the perks of the job. As to their chances with any of the likely runners, most officers would agree that it often depends on how much gold braid you carry on your sleeve.

Humble deck stewards, with no gold braid on their sleeves, are not considered to be in the running. Such a man was James Camb, a good-looking young fellow of thirty-one who worked as a steward on the promenade deck of the *Durban Castle*, now out of South Africa and bound for England. He had learned how to behave correctly towards the passengers, never saying a word out of place, or taking liberties. To have done otherwise would have cost him his job.

But it had not always been so. Previously he had been

in severe trouble for sexually assaulting three women on
board on three separate occasions. Fortunately for him,
none of the women had reported the matter for fear of
marring the voyage still further by having to face Camb
again in front of the captain. If only one of them had,
Camb would have been fired at once and a young woman
named Eileen Gibson would never have been murdered.

A highly sexed man who had now learned to keep his
urges bottled up, his libido was such that it could still lead
him into a great deal of trouble, given the slightest encouragement. That sort of encouragement, which could be
a fatal snare for a man like Camb, was to be placed in his
path in the late October of 1947, soon after Eileen Gibson
came up the gangplank on the first stage of her journey to
Southampton.

An attractive young woman with languorous dark eyes
that held promise of exciting things to any man she might
fall for, Eileen, or Gay Gibson as she was professionally
known, was born in India, but had been educated in
England, where she had served in the Auxiliary Territorial
Service during the war. After expressing a desire to take
up acting as a career, she was transferred to the services'
theatrical company, Stars in Battle Dress. By the time she
left the Army her mind was more set than ever on an
acting career.

Gay had looks, but not a great deal of talent, and the
best she could hope for was work in a minor repertory
company, which meant having to live in cheap lodgings
where the food could be almost as awful as the accommodation. Deciding that her future did not lie in England,
which immediately after the war was drab and depressing,
she decided instead to try her luck in South Africa, where
her father was in business. In South Africa, her theatrical
career had prospered beyond her wildest expectations.
After obtaining work on a radio show, she had the good
fortune to meet an actor-producer named Henry Gilbert,
who gave her the leading role in *The Man With a Load of*

Mischief, a highly successful play by Ashley Dukes, in which she played the lead opposite Eric Boon, the British ex-lightweight boxing champion. When the play unexpectedly seemed in danger of terminating its run, Gay decided that she was ready to tackle the London stage. She booked a passage on the *Durban Castle*, and in due course boarded the ship and was taken to cabin 126 on B deck.

Like most shipboard accommodation, it was sparsely furnished, a single bed more suited to a hospital ward than on an ocean liner being the main item of furniture. It did, however, have a large porthole which let in light and made the cabin seem more cheerful than it really was. It was this porthole which was to play an all important role in the events that followed.

We do not know if Gay had decided to pass the time on board by having an affair. It may well have been in her mind, as a Dutch cap was later found in her luggage. This does not constitute evidence of intent, but it was hardly standard equipment for a sea voyage, especially if you were a nicely brought-up young girl of twenty-one. Certainly, when Camb came up to her one day, she did not treat him with chilly disdain. Far from it. Camb was a personable man with a great deal of surface charm polished in his dealings with passengers. Apart from this, the ship was only half full on that voyage, and any young girl would have been hard put to find a kindred spirit among the geriatric brigade who seemed to make up the main part of the passenger list, so if she did not flirt with him, she may well have given him enough encouragement to think that he was in with more than a chance of 'scoring' with her.

Gay Gibson's tragically short life came to an end in the early hours of 18 October, when they were sailing through the shark-infested waters off the West African coast. Around 5 PM the evening before, Camb had gone down to B deck, where he had been found hovering around Gay's cabin door by Miss Field, the stewardess in charge of cabin quarters. Miss Field had told him sharply to go back to his own part of the ship as this area was forbidden to him. Camb had shrugged and gone on his way, watched by Miss Field, who was debating with herself whether she should report him or not. Finally, she decided to do nothing about it.

When dinner-time came, Gay Gibson appeared in the dining room wearing a black evening gown. After dining at her usual table she went up on deck where she spent some time chatting under the stars with some of the passengers who always shared her table at meal times.

Just before three in the morning, Mr Murray, the night-watchman, was talking to his assistant, Mr Steer, in the first-class galley, when they heard the bell ring for service in one of the cabins. As it was Steer's duty to answer any bells that rang at that time, he went off to deal with the call. On reaching B deck, he was surprised to see that both light calls were on outside cabin 126, the second being for the stewardess. He knocked several times, but there was no answer, although the cabin light shone through the grille in the door. Thinking that something might have happened to Miss Gibson, he was about to go for help when the door suddenly opened a fraction and he caught a glimpse of Camb.

'It's all right,' Camb said, shutting the door quickly, but not before Steer had time to see that he was wearing only a singlet and trousers.

Although Steer had no wish to get another member of the ship's crew into trouble, it was definitely not all right as far as he was concerned. He went away and returned a few minutes later with Murray and they listened for any sound inside the cabin. There was none, and they hurried off to inform the officer on the bridge that night.

'Don't worry about it,' the officer told him, grinning. 'If a passenger chooses to entertain someone in their cabin at this hour, that's their affair. We're not responsible for their morals.'

A ship comes to life early at sea, and Miss Field, the

stewardess, was already busy tidying rooms and making beds before most of the passengers had even had their breakfast. At 7.30 AM she reached cabin 126 and knocked on the door. She received no answer and went in, only to find the cabin empty. She did not find this surprising as Miss Gibson was an early riser and could have gone for an early morning stroll or might have been in the bathroom. As she went to make up the bed she noticed that it was far more disarranged than usual, and assumed that Miss Gibson had spent a restless night. When she made up the bed she noticed there were various stains on the sheets. Miss Field, a conscientious and hard-working woman who took an interest in her passengers, kept an eye out for Miss Gibson until well into the day before eventually becoming worried. She reported the matter to Captain Patey, who immediately ordered the ship to be searched. When she was not to be found, he assumed that she had fallen overboard, and ordered the ship to turn around, though he knew the chances of finding her in these shark-infested waters were slim.

During all the time the ship was being searched and subsequently went back on its tracks, it seems surprising that the officer who was on the bridge in the early hours did not connect Gay's disappearance with the report that Camb had been in Miss Gibson's cabin. Even Steer did not report the matter to Captain Patey until the ship was back on course. Visibly shaken, Patey dismissed Steer, with instructions to keep his mouth shut until the matter had been fully investigated. He then sent for Camb.

'It's not true, sir,' Camb said, when taxed with having been in Gay Gibson's cabin early that morning. 'I went to bed before 12.00 last night. Mr Steer is mistaken if he thinks he saw me.'

'He doesn't think – he knows he saw you,' Captain Patey said brusquely.

'He must have mistaken me for someone else,' Camb said.

Captain Patey remained unconvinced. 'I want you to undergo a medical examination,' he told him. 'It's in your own interests to do so, Camb.'

The next morning Camb reported to the ship's surgeon, who found scratches on his wrists and shoulders.

'Those are easily explained,' Camb said. 'I had an attack of prickly heat the day before and I kept scratching myself to ease the itching.'

This lame excuse merely confirmed the captain's suspicions that Camb had a case to answer. He radioed the Southampton police, who boarded the *Durban Castle* as soon as she docked. Faced with a pair of hard-faced policemen, Camb still tried to deny any knowledge of Gay Gibson, but this time he was not faced with someone like Captain Patey, who had wisely left it to the police to find out the truth. After being grilled for hours, Camb changed his story and then made a formal statement. As a result he was arrested for the murder of Eileen Gibson.

With Camb's statement, we are forced to enter into the realms of supposition, as his account of the events did not equate with the case that was put forward by the Prosecution at his trial. It would have been surprising if it had, as his neck was at stake.

According to Camb, he had encountered Gay late that evening, when he had suggested that she might like him to bring a drink to her cabin. Gay had made some noncommittal answer which Camb had taken to mean that she would not be too upset if he came to her cabin. He had gone there some time later, to find her lying on the bed with a dressing gown on, but nothing underneath it. After a certain amount of foreplay, sexual intercourse had taken place. In the middle of the act, Gay had started foaming at the mouth with some sort of fit and then suddenly died. After trying to resuscitate her, he had panicked and pushed her body through the porthole.

Before going on to relate what later transpired at the trial, it is worth examining his statement. If Gay Gibson had not been expecting Camb, but had suddenly found herself confronted with an intruder bent on rape, why did she not immediately scream out for help or push the bells for the nightwatchman and the stewardess? If she did push the bells immediately, did Camb then rape and strangle her and push her body through the porthole, all within the time that it took the nightwatchman to reach her cabin? It hardly seems likely.

The more likely situation was that Gay had been expecting him, and had only tried to raise the alarm when the situation had suddenly got out of hand. Realizing that Gay was a teaser, and not the compliant partner he had anticipated, Camb had panicked and quickly strangled her before feeding her to the sharks via the porthole.

Another scenario is that she did have a heart attack while having intercourse with Camb. A doctor and a pathologist were produced at the trial, who agreed that this could have happened, given that Gay was in ill health at the time. In evidence produced by the defence, she was subject to fainting fits and had asthma and a number of other complaints that could have caused her death.

The prosecution was to take a quite different line, and supported it with a great deal of damning evidence.

The trial began on 18 March 1948, and was held at Winchester Assizes with Mr Justice Hilbery presiding. The responsibility for the successful prosecution of the case lay with Mr G.D. Roberts, while Mr J.D. Caswell appeared for the defence. Both men were experienced King's Counsels with formidable reputations.

The prosecution opened the proceedings with Mr Roberts drawing attention to the fact that although there was no *corpus delicti*, the absence of a body did not prevent Camb from being tried for murder. He outlined the circumstances of the killing, then point by point began marshalling the evidence which he claimed proved beyond doubt that Camb was guilty of the murder of Eileen Gibson. Apart from a number of stains found on the

sheet, including those of lipstick and dried urine, there
had also been blood stains which had matched the dead
woman's blood group. There was also the Dutch cap
which had been found in the suitcase belonging to Gay
Gibson. Because it had not been used, the prosecution
contended that this proved that she had not consented to
sexual intercourse. The latter was a telling point, but there
was another that does not seem to have been brought up
by the defence at this time. This was the matter of the
lipstick. No woman normally goes to bed with her lipstick
still on. Why was she still wearing it when Camb came to
her cabin? It was three o'clock in the morning, a time
when Gay should have been asleep. One would have
thought that she was still wearing her lipstick because she
was expecting Camb.

It is a small point, but one worth remembering in the
light of a number of other points brought out by the
defence, whose case it was that Gay Gibson had died from
natural causes while engaged in the sexual act. To
strengthen his case Mr Caswell had to prove that Miss
Gibson had been quite happy to jump into bed with any
man she fancied.

When this was put to Miss Gibson's mother, she stoutly
denied it.

'She was one of the finest types of English womanhood,' she declared.

This was coming on a little too strong, but Mrs Gibson's
indignant comment is understandable. No mother likes to
see her daughter's reputation being dragged through the
mire in public.

Mr Caswell had no such qualms. He put forward the
names of a number of men whom, he claimed, Miss
Gibson had known intimately. When Mrs Gibson denied
that her daughter had slept with any of them, Mr Caswell
asked casually, 'Have you heard of a man named Charles
Sventonski?'

'Yes,' Mrs Gibson said. 'He was one of Eileen's friends.

He was very kind to her. He paid her passage to England and gave her £500.' Seeing the triumphant gleam in Mr Caswell's eyes, she added quickly, 'It was a business arrangement. Mr Sventonski had great faith in my daughter's talents.'

'I'm sure he had,' Mr Caswell murmured. 'But did you think it right that your daughter should have accepted such a large sum of money from a man who had known her for only a short time?'

'I saw no harm in it,' Mrs Gibson said defiantly. 'She had every intention of paying it back.'

Having tried to sow the seed in the jury's mind that Eileen Gibson was a woman of loose morals, Mr Caswell then put Camb on the stand and led him through his story, which was much the same as the one he had told the police in Southampton. No doubt he had rehearsed it many times in his cell while awaiting his trial.

Still hammering away at the supposition that Gay had died while having sex with the accused, Mr Caswell then produced a number of witnesses from South Africa, who all agreed with him that Gay Gibson had been a sick young lady who had suffered from a variety of rather alarming complaints. One witness even claimed that during one of her asthmatic attacks he had seen her lips turn blue. This, coupled with all the other evidence from the South African witnesses, should have been enough to prove that Eileen Gibson could have died from a heart attack while having sex with Camb. It was still not enough to save him.

If Mr Caswell had proved to be a most able KC, then Mr Roberts was to prove a deadly one.

After leading Camb into admitting he was an inveterate liar, Mr Roberts asked him a seemingly innocent question that effectively scotched any chance Camb might have had of getting away with a verdict of manslaughter.

'When sexual intercourse took place with Miss Gibson, what were your positions?'

'I was lying on top of Miss Gibson,' Camb told him. 'We were face to face.'

Mr Roberts was to come back to this later when he was questioning Professor Webster, one of the witnesses for the defence. The stain of dried urine on the top sheet was his next point. He put it to Professor Webster that in cases of strangulation, was it not a fact that the bladder invariably discharged its contents. When Professor Webster agreed it was, Mr Roberts looked significantly at the jury. The inference was clear. If Camb had been lying on top of Miss Gibson, the urine would have ejected over him and not the sheet, and he must therefore have been standing over her and strangling her when the bladder had discharged its contents.

The jury took the point. They had already decided they disliked Camb, who had been far too calm and in control of himself during the trial. After an unfavourable summing-up from Justice Hilbery, the jury were sent out to reach a decision. They were back within three-quarters of an hour with a verdict of guilty. Despite the number of telling points that Mr Caswell had made in Camb's favour, one can understand why they reached their decision in a remarkably short space of time. Although Mr Caswell had proved there was a possibility that Eileen Gibson had died from natural causes, this had been completely negated by Mr Roberts's final and most damning disclosure about the ejection of the contents of the bladder.

Camb's statement that he had got rid of the body as he did because he had panicked was ignored. It was a plea of mitigation that had been used too many times before, though sometimes with more successful results.

Camb was found guilty on 22 March 1948, and was sentenced to be hanged. This should have been the end of the matter, with Camb being executed early one morning. This time, however, Camb was in luck. While his appeal was pending, the Criminal Justice Bill, proposing the substitution of life imprisonment for hanging, was being debated in Parliament. The Home Secretary decided that while the issue was in doubt, all pending executions should be commuted to life imprisonment.

It was still not the last we were to hear of Camb. He was released on licence in 1959. He then disappeared from public view until 1967, when he was arrested and convicted of indecently assaulting a young girl. Considering his criminal record, it is little short of amazing that he got away with nothing more than being put on probation for two years. Two years later, while working in Scotland, he was up in court again, this time for indecent behaviour with three schoolgirls. His licence was revoked and he was sent back to prison to complete his sentence.

A MOTHER'S TENDER CONCERN

Elizabeth Duncan, Augustine Baldonado
and Luis Moya

American murder case 1958

To see Mrs Elizabeth Duncan walking past the shops in downtown Santa Barbara, California, accompanied by a frail old lady in her seventies, one might be excused for thinking they were two elderly ladies out on a shopping expedition. In a sense, they were out shopping, but not for something like a hat or a sensible pair of shoes. What they were looking for was a killer who could be relied on to dispose of Mrs Duncan's new daughter-in-law, who had dared to marry her son Frank, thereby putting an end to their cosy relationship which appeared to verge on the incestuous to the outsider. 'He would never *dare* to marry,' she had been known to say on various occasions, in tones that brooked no opposition from the person she was hectoring at the time. But Frank had turned out not to be quite the pliable person that Mrs Duncan had thought him to be. In defiance of her wishes he had married an attractive nurse named Olga Kupczyk, the daughter of a railroad foreman.

Events leading up to the marriage had not been without traumatic situations for all concerned. Frank was a lawyer of some standing in the local community, and he was becoming uncomfortably aware that his mother was causing him embarrassment, mainly because of her habit of turning up at every court where he appeared and vigorously applauding every speech he made. He was fast becoming a laughing stock and the object of commiseration among his colleagues at the Bar. Unable to stand any more of this stifling mother love which was threatening to ruin his career and was bringing him to the edge of a nervous breakdown, Frank decided the time had come at last to free himself of his mother.

This, as he soon found out, was more easily said than done. Quietly but firmly, he told her that things could not go on the way they had done before, and that he had his own life to lead – which did not include Mrs Duncan dogging his footsteps wherever he went. Faced with a revolt on her hands, Mrs Duncan began screaming hysterically at him, while reminding him what he owed her – which was actually very little. When Frank remained firm, she went home and took an overdose of sleeping pills.

An uncharitable person might be of the opinion that by taking a carefully calculated overdose, Mrs Duncan was merely trying to bring her son back into line, and once the grief-stricken Frank had rushed to her side, full of contrition, there would be a touching reconciliation, and all would be well again. Ironically, the way matters turned out it was the worst thing she could have done. When the panic-stricken Frank arrived at the hospital, one of the first people he saw was Olga Kupczyk. They fell in love, almost on sight, and Mrs Duncan was forced to watch their love blossom while she lay fuming in bed.

When his mother was back home again, Frank decided not to tell her just how serious his feelings were about Olga, and Mrs Duncan began to relax, thinking that his interest in the girl had been only of a temporary nature. In the meantime, Frank continued to see Olga until the day came when she announced she was pregnant. Realizing that the inevitable could not be put off any longer, Frank confronted his mother with the news and told her of his intention to marry Olga. There was another terrible scene which culminated in Mrs Duncan storming out of the house in search of Olga. When she eventually found her, she told the startled girl that if she dared to marry her son, she would kill her.

Knowing that they were dealing with someone whose actions bordered on those of a mad woman, Olga and

Frank quietly married without Mrs Duncan's knowledge. This led to an impossible situation for Frank, where he spent the evening with his wife before returning to sleep at his mother's house late at night. It was the sort of situation which has been used in several film comedies, dealing with a bigamist running to and fro between two women. With Mrs Duncan as one of the central players it was far from being a comedy.

It did not take Mrs Duncan long to find out about the marriage, and from then on she waged a war of attrition against Olga and Frank. This included continually harassing Olga in the street, or landing unexpectedly on their doorstep to harangue Olga, much to the poor girl's embarrassment and fury. In this, as with all matters concerning his mother, Frank does not seem to have been the pillar of support he should have been to his wife.

But if Frank was weak-willed, his wife was not when it came to holding her ground against Mrs Duncan. Instead of packing her bags and departing, she stayed where she was, hoping that her mother-in-law would eventually come to terms with the situation. What she had not reckoned with was Mrs Duncan's iron determination to get rid of her – even if it meant resorting to murder.

It was at this point that Mrs Duncan decided to enlist the aid of Mrs Emma Short, a hard-faced widow who looked more normal than she really was. Then in the first stages of senile dementia, Emma listened to her friend's plans for murder without seeing anything morally wrong in them, though she did gather her failing wits together to say at one time that she didn't really approve of what Mrs Duncan was intending to do.

After dismissing the idea of disfiguring Olga with acid as not being final enough, Mrs Duncan then went on to outline the first of her plans. This involved Emma luring Olga to her home, and while she was there, Mrs Duncan would spring out of the cupboard and strangle her with a piece of rope. The body was then to be left hanging until late that evening, when she would take it to the sea and throw it off one of the wharfs with a large rock attached to it.

'You're not paying attention to what I'm saying,' Mrs Duncan said sharply, when she noticed that her friend's attention seemed to be wandering.

Emma brought herself back to the present with an effort. 'Yes, I am. I don't like your idea of leaving a body for me to look after all day.'

Mrs Duncan could see that her friend was going to be difficult, but she persevered. 'Then how's this for an idea ...?'

Her next plan seemed just as impractical. 'We'll find ourselves a killer who will do the job for us,' she announced.

Emma looked doubtful. 'Where would you find one?' she asked, in a rare display of common sense.

'I know just where to go,' Mrs Duncan said triumphantly. 'Get your coat and hat and follow me.'

Mrs Duncan had remembered that her son had defended a family of Mexican immigrants who owned the Tropical Cafe in the Mexican quarter of Santa Barbara. Like so many of the bars and cafes in that area, it was a sleazy little business frequented by all manner of dangerous-looking characters who looked as if they would slit their mother's throat for a handful of dollars. It was to this cafe that Mrs Duncan made her way with Emma tottering gamely in her wake. Mrs Esquivel, the matriarch of the family, was behind the counter when they came in.

'You will remember me, I'm sure,' Mrs Duncan said. 'My son successfully defended your family when they were up in court for receiving stolen goods.'

Mrs Esquivel looked at her warily. 'What can I do for you?'

'My daughter-in-law is blackmailing me, and soon she will start doing the same to my poor son,' Mrs Duncan said. 'She must be removed. Perhaps you could give us the name of someone who would be prepared to deal with the matter for me – at a price?'

It is safe to assume that Mrs Esquivel had never before been asked to supply the name of a 'hit' man to a couple of old ladies, but she rose admirably to the occasion. 'I know of two boys who might help,' she said, after some thought.

'Could you please arrange for us to meet them?' Mrs Duncan asked.

'Return tomorrow afternoon and they will be waiting for you,' Mrs Esquivel said.

Thanking her, Mrs Duncan swept out with the faithful Emma in tow. The two of them returned the next day, when they met two young Mexicans named Augustine Baldonado and Luis Moya. Emma was sent to sit at another table while Mrs Duncan put her proposition to them.

'How much?' Moya asked.

'$3,000,' Mrs Duncan said, plucking the figure out of the air.

'Make it 6,000,' Moya said. '3,000 up front and the balance afterwards.'

'I haven't got that sort of money with me,' Mrs Duncan said. After a great deal of haggling, she reluctantly parted with $175, promising to deliver the balance as soon as the job was done.

'We've got a real bargain with those two,' Mrs Duncan said happily to her friend as they made their way home. What she had actually obtained were the services of two bungling young criminals who were so desperate for money that they had agreed to murder for a trifling advance sum which amounted to less than £55 each.

It may seem incredible to the average European mind that they were prepared to kill for so little. To understand why one has to comprehend something of the Mexican mentality. Octavia Paz, the eminent Mexican poet and philosopher, supplies the answer in his *The Labyrinth of*

Solitude, a highly perceptive study of the Mexican character, which points out that to the average Mexican life is nothing, therefore death is nothing. Such fatalism has always been part of the Mexican philosophy, especially where the poor and underprivileged of the nation were always kept in a state of near servitude by the ruling classes, a policy handed down by the Spanish and perpetuated by the rich landowners who had been followed by a long line of dictators posing as liberators. All of them, without exception, had been supported by the Church, whose baneful influence has been in Mexico since the days of the conquistadores. Moya and Baldonado were very much products of their society.

Having agreed to carry out the killing, the two young Mexicans wasted no time in getting the job done. After hiring a broken-down old Chevrolet and borrowing a pistol from one of their friends, they then drove down to the address which Mrs Duncan had given them. Leaving Baldonado in the car, Moya hurried up the stairs to the apartment where Frank and his wife lived.

'I have brought your husband home, señora,' he said when Olga came to the door, 'I found him drunk in a bar and have brought him home to you. But I need a little help to get him up here . . .'

If Olga had been less flustered by Moya's unexpected arrival on her doorstep she might have been less trusting than she was. Frank was not a heavy drinker, and if he ever did go into a bar, it was not one likely to be frequented by a suspicious-looking character such as Moya. Instead, she accompanied Moya downstairs to the waiting Baldonado, who was lying on the back seat, hoping that in the darkness Olga Duncan would take him for her husband.

The ruse, elementary though it was, worked. Opening the door for her, Moya stood back while Olga came forward and peered into the car. 'Frank?' she called out softly. Before she could utter another word Moya whipped out his pistol and struck her with a savage blow to the head. As she slumped forward he bundled her into the car beside Baldonado and then ran to the driver's seat and drove off. The actual kidnap had taken no more than twenty seconds.

It had been the intention of the two killers to finish off Olga in some quiet spot and then bury the body somewhere near the Mexican border. As events turned out it was not to be as simple as that.

While they were speeding in the direction of the Mexican border, Olga suddenly regained consciousness and began screaming for help. Baldonado immediately began to grapple with her, attempting to fix his hands around her throat so that he could strangle her. Frantic with fear, she managed to beat him off and then tried to reach for the door handle, at which point Moya stopped the car, and leaning over the seat, managed to strike her several vicious blows to the head. With blood streaming down the side of her face she collapsed to the floor of the car.

Badly shaken, the two men were now anxious to get rid of the body as soon as possible. Abandoning the idea of making for the Mexican border, they headed for the nearby mountains. Eventually finding a large ditch off the main highway, they tipped Olga's body out of the car, only to find that she was still breathing, and, moreover, showing signs of life again. This time they made sure she was finally silenced for all time. First, Baldonado strangled her and then Moya found a large rock which he crashed down on her head, spattering their clothing with even more blood. 'Now we bury her,' Moya muttered.

When they returned to the car, it was to find that in their haste to get the job done they had forgotten to bring a shovel with them. '*Madre de Dios*,' Moya said 'What do we do now?'

There was only one thing they could do, and that was to bury the body with their bare hands. In total darkness they both scrabbled away at the earth until they had dug a hole

deep enough to take the body. Having finally disposed of
Olga – hopefully to lie undisturbed for years in her
shallow grave – Moya and Baldonado hurried back to the
car and drove off into the night. Nothing had gone quite
as they had planned – and worse was to come.

As they drove back to Santa Barbara, they discussed the
balance of the money that was due to them from Mrs
Duncan. 'Let's hope the old lady will pay up,' Baldonado
muttered.

'Don't worry,' Moya said confidently. 'She'll pay.'

Meanwhile, Frank had returned home to find the apartment empty, without even a note from Olga telling him
that she had just slipped out on an errand and would be
back soon. Frank was worried, and with some cause.
Santa Barbara had never been a safe town and had always
had more than its fair share of murders and robberies with
violence. After waiting for some time, hoping that Olga
would come home, Frank finally decided to phone the
police, who came round almost immediately. After looking
round the apartment and seeing no signs of a struggle,
they left, reassuring Frank that his wife would probably
return shortly and, if not, they would soon find her.

Two days later, Mrs Duncan received a phone call from
Moya. 'We have completed the work you asked us to do,'
Moya said. 'When shall we meet to collect the money you
owe us?'

As an elderly housewife of sixty-two with no contacts in
the criminal world, Mrs Duncan had achieved something
of a miracle in finding two men who had been prepared to
kill for her. What she could not do was conjure up the sort
of money she now owed them. Instead, she had prepared
a story which she hoped would keep them at bay. 'The
police have already been to see me about Olga,' she lied.
'If I draw that sort of money out of the bank they'll
become suspicious. I've $200 in the house. That will have
to do until things quieten down.' Moya reluctantly agreed,
and they arranged to meet.

Mrs Duncan arrived at the meeting place accompanied by Emma, who seems to have been made privy to every step that her friend had made from the beginning. Mrs Duncan handed over the envelope without a word and then marched off with Emma trailing in her wake. When they had gone, Moya opened the envelope and, to his fury, found that it contained only $120. Cursing, he went home to tell Baldonado that they had been conned.

It turns out that Elizabeth Duncan seems to have spent most of her life conning men out of their money. She had either married or lived with a considerable number in her younger days and there had been no love on her part in any relationship made for the money she might get out of the unfortunate man she had battened on. Considering the sort of woman she was, it is surprising that she had not killed any of them off for the insurance money.

As it was, in the end she had not done well for herself, ending her days as a hard-up old woman with no friends, except for Emma, and of course, her son Frank, who was to remain loyal to the end.

After receiving a number of threatening phone calls from the killers, Mrs Duncan embarked on a course of action which she hoped would send them fleeing from the area once they knew what she had done. With supreme confidence in her ability to deceive the police, she marched into the local station and informed them that she was being blackmailed by two Mexicans who had threatened to kill her and Frank if she did not pay up. As far as Mrs Duncan was concerned, her story was a plausible one as Frank had frequent dealings with criminals in his work.

But this time Mrs Duncan had overreached herself. Listening to her story, which had more holes in it than the proverbial sieve, the police became suspicious. This was intensified once they began their investigation with a few discreet enquiries among the neighbours. They learned that Mrs Duncan had detested her daughter-in-law, and that Emma Short was Mrs Duncan's only friend. When

Emma was brought in for questioning, she talked freely to the police. Like most people suffering from senile dementia, she had her good days when she was fairly rational, and this was one of them.

The two detectives who were questioning her listened incredulously to the story she had to tell. When she had finished the two of them looked at each other, and then one of them said, 'You say that you didn't approve of Mrs Duncan's plans to have her daughter-in-law murdered?'

'Of course I didn't,' Emma snapped.

'Then why didn't you report the matter before it was too late?'

Emma looked vaguely into space. 'I didn't think it was necessary,' she said.

From then on, events moved swiftly. The two young Mexicans were arrested and eventually put on trial before a jury which listened with fascinated horror to this story of twisted mother love. They brought in a verdict of murder in the first degree for all three. As is the American Way, which seems to allow countless appeals on one pretext or another before a condemned person takes the final walk to their execution, it was not until 6 August 1962 that Moya and Baldonado went to the gas chamber, where they died side by side. Mrs Duncan went soon after, despite Frank's last desperate attempt to find a legal loophole which could have led to another stay of execution.

Few men would have taken the trouble with a mother who had been responsible for the murder of their wife.

AN IMPOSSIBLE CASE

Tony Mancini

English murder case 1934

In the 1930s the Sussex seaside town of Brighton had the reputation of being a rather raffish resort where couples from London came to spend an illicit weekend. Others saw it merely as the ideal place to spend a fortnight by the sea. As such it had much to recommend it. Apart from the sea, on which the sun always seemed to shine, it had two piers, the famous Sherry's dance hall where the young and the not-so-young used to flock daily and the Royal Pavilion where one could idle away the odd hour wandering around the Oriental fantasy designed by John Nash for the Prince Regent, as well as the picture palaces and a racetrack. It was the latter which attracted a large criminal element, giving the resort a slightly sinister underside and conveying a sense of danger to the town's visitors. Apart from this hard core of professional criminals there was an army of petty thieves who earned a living by stealing or picking pockets, or by prostitution and pimping. It was to this group that Tony Mancini belonged.

Mancini was not a vicious criminal like Pinky in Graham Greene's novel *Brighton Rock*, which for the first time showed the seamy side of Brighton, known to only few of the holidaymakers. Mancini did, however, have a record of petty crime, and it was therefore fairly inevitable that he should gravitate to a busy town like Brighton and become part of the flotsam and jetsam that gathered like scum around the perimeters of Brighton's professional criminal class.

Mancini was born Cecil Lois England and was brought

up in Newcastle-on-Tyne in Northumberland, but was educated in Hertfordshire. After he left school he joined the Air Force and he became just one more of the many trying to escape civilian life and its attendant difficulties of trying to exist in a world without even a welfare state to make life fractionally easier for the needy.

By the time he returned to civilian life, two years later, the country was still recovering from the General Strike of 1926. In those times it was difficult for even a skilled artisan to get work, let alone Tony Mancini, who was ill equipped to get any sort of work beyond that of clearing tables in some sleazy cafe with fly-blown windows and a menu designed to accommodate the pockets of the poor. Not surprisingly, he turned to petty crime, but had no success at that either and was soon caught and given a jail sentence. He came out of prison in 1933 and became known in various haunts around Soho as Tony Mancini, a name he must have thought more appropriate than his own as he was trying to get work as a waiter in a restaurant in Leicester Square. He met an ex-dancer named Violette Kaye, and though it was hardly the Romance of the Year, they got on well enough to live together in comparative harmony.

The pair eventually found themselves in Brighton, where they rented a basement flat at 44 Park Crescent. Like so many of the town's streets, it had once been more gracious-looking than it was when Tony and Violette took up residence there. The interiors of many of the houses were still more imposing than the frontages, with Doric pillars in drawing-rooms which went through to the backs of the houses whose wrought-iron balconies overlooked small gardens which led into a small private part shared by all the residents. Although it was going through a period when it was becoming bed-sit land for transients, Park Crescent had the merit of being quiet, though the bustling Lewes Road shopping area was only a few minutes away.

It suited Tony Mancini as it was near to the racetrack,

where he had hoped to make a living. Unfortunately, it did not work out that way. Tony was neither slick nor self-assured enough to have ever become a member of the racetrack fraternity, even as a runner for one of the bookies. The little money they had saved while working in Soho soon dwindled away, and Violette decided to take up prostitution while Tony found himself a job as a part-time waiter at the Skylark Cafe which was situated on Brighton's Undercliff. It was one of those places which did a roaring trade in the summer, supplying tea trays for the beach and lunch for as little as a shilling. Though it was not exactly a step up in the world for Mancini, it did provide some sort of income when Violette's trade was slack and every penny counted. When Violette's trade was brisk Mancini was careful to be out, and when the weather was bad, he stayed quietly out of the way in the other room until Violette's client had departed. It was a sordid sort of existence which neither of them could have enjoyed, but they kept together and seldom quarrelled from all accounts.

Inevitably, Violette's way of life began to take its toll and she started to drink heavily and take drugs. Mancini was now living in a pressure-cooker atmosphere in which their poverty, his own pent-up emotions and Violette's descent into a private hell of her own were all building up to such an extent that something had to give soon. It came on 10 May when they had a violent quarrel before Mancini went to work. That afternoon Violette was due to entertain a client named Charles Moore, one of the local bookies. Suddenly finding himself with some pressing business to attend to, he sent his assistant around to the house to cancel the appointment. Violette came to the door and Moore's assistant gave her the message, noting that she seemed in a 'distressed condition' and was obviously glad to be rid of him as soon as possible. Before he went, Moore's assistant thought he heard the sound of voices coming from the flat, but took no notice of it at the

time, thinking that Violette was entertaining a client. He
was to remember it later when he read that a body had
been found in a trunk. It had been identified as the
remains of Violette Kaye.

The next day, Mancini went to work as usual at the
Skylark Cafe, where he told other members of the staff
that Violette had taken herself off to Paris to work as a
dancer in Montmartre. It did not occur to any of them
that Violette was somewhat over the hill to have found
herself a job in Paris (except perhaps in a brothel) and
they accepted Mancini's story without comment. The next
day Violette's sister in London received a telegram
purporting to be from Violette, which read: *Going abroad.
Good job. Sailing Sunday. Will write. Vi.*

On the Saturday of the same week, Mancini went along
to the bustling street market in Gardener Street, where he
found just what he was looking for – a large second-hand
trunk. He had taken along with him one of the waiters
from the Skylark Cafe, and together they managed to get
it back to the flat in Park Crescent. Having thanked his
friend on the doorstep, Mancini took the trunk inside the
basement flat and then went upstairs to give notice to his
landlady. After spending the afternoon packing, he left to
take up residence in another basement flat he had already
found for himself in Kemp Street.

Once he was settled in, Mancini was careful to keep out
of the way of his new landlady. She did not find this
unusual as she was not particularly interested in her
tenants, who all came and went with monotonous regularity. He had only been there for about a week when the
other tenants began to complain of a vile smell that was
beginning to permeate the whole house. Their complaints
rose in proportion to the ever-increasing odour until the
landlady was forced to go down to Mancini's flat. While
she was there she noticed a dark fluid emanating from the
base of a large trunk in the corner of the room.

'It must be coming from the bottle of furniture polish I

haven't had time yet to unpack,' Mancini told her. 'It's obviously broken. I'll deal with it as soon as you've gone.'

'See that you do,' his landlady said. 'And do something about that awful smell.'

Mancini must have got busy with disinfectant as soon as she left as the complaints ceased.

If it had not been for the discovery of a dismembered body found in a trunk left at Brighton Station, there is no telling what Mancini might have done in the future. As must now be obvious, Mancini had another body of his very own hidden in the trunk in his living room.

The body found at Brighton Station had been found on 17 June and had been deposited there eleven days before. It was without its head and legs, which made identification difficult, if not impossible, but the police did their best. The first thing they did was interview hundreds of people, including Tony Mancini, who was soon cleared of being a likely suspect. To this day, neither the identity of the woman in the trunk at Brighton Station has ever been established, nor the murderer ever caught.

As for Mancini, the first thing he did after the police released him was to head for the station, where he caught the next train for London, leaving his unfortunate land-lady to find the mouldering remains of Violette Kaye in the trunk. Having been there for over a month, the condition of the body was such as to send her screaming from the room.

The police now had two bodies on their hands, but at least with the arrival of the second one at the mortuary, they knew the man they were after and the identity of the dead woman. An alert was put out to all ports, and Mancini's description circulated to police stations throughout the country. Even so, it was not until 17 July that he was recognized by a Lewisham policeman, who arrested him as he was walking along the Maidstone Road.

'I'm the man you're looking for,' Mancini admitted

freely. 'But I didn't murder her.'

According to the statement he made later on, he had come home to find Violette Kaye lying murdered on the bed with wounds to her head and blood on the sheets. Knowing that he had a police record, and thinking he would be arrested and found guilty for a crime he hadn't committed, he had decided to conceal the body until he had decided how he was going to dispose of it. 'As God is my witness,' he concluded, 'I don't know who killed her. My only crime was that I kept the body hidden.'

At this point it is worth examining the validity of Mancini's story. We know that he was on good terms with Violette until she began drinking and taking drugs, and even then he did nothing more than try to remonstrate with her. Although he was not too happy about her taking up prostitution, he was a pragmatist who knew that without the income she brought in from her trade, they would probably starve. Like all prostitutes dealing with the lower end of the market, she took dreadful risks, and it is quite possible that she had been murdered by one of her clients, or so it seemed at the time.

On the other hand, for a man who was supposed to have been panic-stricken on finding the body, Mancini's subsequent behaviour was that of someone who knew what he was doing. He not only spread the story of Violette suddenly taking off to Paris, but also remembered to send a telegram to her sister, telling her the same story.

In the minds of the public and popular press there were no doubts about his guilt. The public jeered him at the hearing, and although the press did not come out with a statement to the effect that he was guilty, many of the crime reporters writing on the subject slanted their articles to make him appear in an unfavourable light, which made him appear guilty, if only by implication.

But for once in his life, Mancini was lucky. Before he was committed for trial at the Sussex Assizes he had obtained the services of a Brighton solicitor named Mr

F.H. Carpenter, who was on good terms with the clerk to the already legendary Mr Norman Birkett, who agreed to defend Mancini.

Why did he take the case when the result of the trial seemed a foregone conclusion? Even his clerk had been reluctant to take the brief, knowing that a defeat in court could only lead to a lessening of Norman Birkett's present reputation. It may have been because he relished challenging yet again the evidence of his old opponent, the pathologist Sir Bernard Spilsbury, whose pronouncements in the witness box were generally received with unquestioning acceptance by the judge and jury. His seeming infallability had irked Norman Birkett, who claimed on one occasion in court, and with some truth, that 'it will be an evil day when in the criminal courts, merely because of attainments, distinctions and experience, the word of any expert is accepted as final and conclusive ...'

It may be that he relished a battle in which he had to fight against seemingly impossible odds. If that was the case, he was to give the most brilliant performance of his career in his fight to save Mancini from the gallows.

The trial began on 10 December 1934, with Mr J.D. Cassels and Mr Quintin Hogg appearing for the Crown, while Mr Norman Birkett was supported by Mr John Flower, KC, and Mr Eric Neve. Soon after Mr Cassels had opened the case for the prosecution it soon became obvious that Mancini and his more than able defenders had an uphill task before them.

Everything seemed against Mancini from the start. He was a coarse-faced man with jug ears, who could easily have passed as Italian or Maltese. This may seem irrelevant, but it was far from being so in those days. Mancini came to trial when racial prejudice was rife. One has only to look at the popular fiction of the time to see just how virulent this prejudice was. In the famous Bulldog Drummond adventure stories, Jews were depicted with heavy Semitic features behaving in much the same manner as

they were to be portrayed in the Nazi paper *Der Stürm,*
while Italians were seen as greasy 'wops'. It was bad
enough for Mancini and Norman Birkett to have to face
this sort of prejudice in a jury; when it was coupled with
the mass of damning evidence against Mancini, who sat in
the dock looking cowed and the very picture of the seedy
petty criminal he was, one would not have given much for
his chances.

Two of the most telling points against him were a
charred hammer which had been found among the
rubbish at Park Crescent, and the fact that he had once
knocked unconscious a man who had been trying to
blackmail him, thereby proving that he was capable of
violence when provoked. The question was to have added
significance when witnesses testified that in conversation
Mancini had said that the best way to deal with a difficult
woman was to take a hammer to her, at which point Mr
Cassels had given the jury a long, meaningful look. The
remark may have been no more than a piece of bombastic
talk among friends, but Norman Birkett did not bother to
make that point. He had more telling evidence in his
client's favour to bring to the jury's attention.

The finding of the hammer seemed an even more
serious matter – that is until Norman Birkett went to work
on the evidence of Sir Bernard Spilsbury, who was no
longer so sure of himself as he had been when he had first
examined the hammer before the trial. A cold, aloof man,
he had first made his reputation at the age of thirty-three,
when his evidence had put a rope around the neck of Dr
Crippen. His reputation had been dented a couple of
years previously, when Sir Patrick Hastings had merci-
lessly torn his evidence to shreds during the trial of Mrs
Elvira Barney, who had been accused of shooting her
lover, Scott Stephen. He was about to receive another
trouncing at the hands of Norman Birkett.

When he took the stand, bracing himself to resist
Birkett's deadly questions, Spilsbury was no longer the

man he had been when he helped send Patrick Mahon to the gallows (see 'The Love Bungalow'.) His evidence in murder trials was now viewed with more suspicion, and seen as invested with dogmatic and narrow views that brooked no other opinion. When he had first examined the hammer found in Park Crescent, it had been Spilsbury's opinion that it was the weapon used to kill Violette Kaye. Under Birkett's insistent questioning he now had to admit that he could not even tell which end of the hammer had been used. As there were no blood stains on the hammer, Spilsbury's last admission made the so-called evidence of the hammer virtually useless.

'Is it not possible that the depressed fracture of the skull could have been caused by a fall down the stairs at Park Crescent?' Birkett enquired.

Sir Bernard Spilsbury had to admit that it was possible.

Birkett next dealt with the question of some blood stains that had been found on the prisoner's suit. Although the prosecution had been unable to identify the blood group it was obvious that the members of the jury were convinced that the blood belonged to Violette Kaye. It was at this point that Birkett produced a surprise witness – a Brighton tailor who was able to swear that he had supplied Mancini with the suit *after* the murder had been committed.

Having left the jury beginning to waver for the first time over the question of Mancini's guilt, Birkett then called Detective Inspector Donaldson of Scotland Yard to the stand. Like so many other people in this case, he was convinced that Mancini was guilty.

'Inspector, I believe you were called in at the beginning of this case.'

'Yes, sir.'

Birkett pointed a finger in Mancini's direction. 'This man is a blackguard, isn't he?'

'Yes, sir. I should describe him as such.'

'An idle, worthless man without morals or principles?'

'Yes, sir. I think that sums him up.'

'A man with previous convictions?'

'That is so.'

By now, both the inspector and Mancini must have been wondering whose side Birkett was on. Ignoring the prisoner's worried look, Birkett continued to pursue his line of questioning, which seemed to destroy whatever Mancini's chances were of an acquittal – that is until he came to his key question.

'A man, though, with no conviction or charge of violence?'

'None, sir.'

Having torn to shreds his client's reputation, which had already been demolished by the prosecution anyway, he then indulged himself in a piece of showmanship which was intended to destroy the veracity of much of the press reporting on the trial. Picking up a national newspaper which lay to hand, he studied one of the pages for a few moments and then looked up at the inspector. 'There is a paragraph in this newspaper that says the prisoner was previously charged and convicted of violence. According to your previous answer this is completely untrue.'

'Yes, sir. It is quite untrue.'

Once more Birkett had scored a point off one of the witnesses for the prosecution. So far, he had totally discredited the evidence of Sir Bernard Spilsbury and made the Crown's key witness seem useless, and not only that, he had also proved that the press reporting on the case had been biased in favour of the Crown. His master stroke was yet to come at the end of his closing speech.

Mr J.D. Cassels continued to hammer away at what was already known and admitted by the defence, and tried to prove that the prisoner was a liar and a man who had attempted to get an innocent party to provide him with an alibi. This was a 17-year-old girl named Doris Saville, who claimed that she had met Mancini soon after he had left the police station and that he had tried to persuade her to provide him with an alibi.

'What exactly is an alibi?' Birkett asked politely when it was his turn to cross-examine her.

Doris Saville hesitated and then shook her head. 'I don't know,' she admitted.

Nothing that Birkett did after this trial was to match the brilliance of his closing speech on this occasion. Throughout the trial he had made a point of stressing time and again that Mancini was an unsavoury character without any redeeming features and, by doing so, had taken much of the sting out of the case for the prosecution. More important, he had proved more than a reasonable motive for Mancini not going to the police when he discovered the body. As he was careful to point out, a man of Mancini's criminal background knew that he would have been arrested and convicted for the murder. 'In those circumstances,' Birkett told the jury, 'a man with his background could all too easily commit himself to an irrevocable act of folly.'

He also brought to the attention of the jury the lack of motive. 'When Mancini was in the witness box I wanted to hear some suggestion as to why he had done it. There has been no word on this vital question.'

Starting from a position where Mancini's case seemed hopeless, Birkett's defence had turned what could have been a resounding defeat into one of his most triumphant victories in court. The jury went out for two and a half hours before it returned with a verdict of not guilty.

When Mancini walked out of court that day a free man, most people thought they had heard the last of him. Apart from a brief spell when he capitalized on his notoriety by appearing in a travelling show where he was billed as 'The Infamous Brighton Trunk Murder Man', he was not heard of again until 1976, when the readers of the *News of the World* were startled to read the following headline in their paper: 'I Got Away With Murder'. In the article that followed they read how Mancini had decided to break his silence and admit that he was responsible for the murder of Violette Kaye. One asks oneself why he bothered after allowing forty-two years to pass before he came forward. The answer being that he was hard up and knew he was safe, since a person cannot be tried for the same murder twice. According to his story he had killed her unintentionally when they were quarrelling, and he had repeatedly banged her head against a fender, only to realize too late that he had murdered her. He gave another interview later on, in which his story varied in certain details, but was essentially the same in the description of the way in which he killed her.

It is ironic that one of Norman Birkett's most successful defences was made on behalf of a criminal who was guilty of the crime as charged.

THE KILLER IN THE NIGHT

Sam Sheppard

American murder case 1954

This was a murder case in which not only the accused but a number of innocent people suffered. The accused, Sam Sheppard, was eventually acquitted, only to spend the rest of his life on a downward spiral, from being a highly respected doctor, to becoming an all-in wrestler before he died, shunned by those who once regarded him so highly. In all this he resembled one of those tortured film heroes, such as Laurence Olivier in *Carrie*, who plunges from riches to abject poverty before shuffling into the night. Only this story was for real.

The story of Sam Sheppard began on the night of 3 July 1954, soon after the family had retired to bed after having spent a pleasant evening entertaining friends to dinner. Within the next few hours Sam's well-ordered life turned into a living nightmare.

Until that night, his life had been that of a typical well-off and well-connected member of the medical profession. His father was Dr Richard Sheppard, a general surgeon and osteopath and the founder of the Cleveland Bay Hospital, where Sam worked as a neurosurgeon. While there he met and married Marilyn Reese and bought a nice house close to the hospital and overlooking Lake Erie. In due course they had a son named Sean. His arrival completing one of those upwardly mobile family units representing the American Dream, where money, social position and conservative values play such an important part.

On the night of the murder, Marilyn Sheppard had gone up to the bedroom, leaving her husband on the couch watching television. As with most late-night shows, the programme he was watching had a soporophic effect and he was soon fast asleep. According to his testament in court later, he was awakened by the sound of his wife screaming. He rushed upstairs, only to be struck a vicious blow on the back of the head as he entered the bedroom. When he came to, he saw his wife lying on the bed with blood pouring from her head and spreading into a large stain on the pillows and sheets. More blood had spattered the walls behind the bed, and Sheppard saw at a glance that the room had been ransacked.

He was about to go and see if his son was safe when he heard a noise below. He ran downstairs, where he was in time to see someone disappearing out of the back door. Chasing after the intruder, he caught up with him on the beach, only to be knocked unconscious for the second time.

When he recovered, instead of phoning the police, he called a neighbour and friend, J. Spencer Houk, the mayor of the town. He told him what had happened, and Mr and Mrs Houk came over to the house within minutes, where they found Sheppard slumped in a chair looking gaunt-eyed and still dizzy from the blows he had received on the head. Sheppard pointed speechlessly to the upstairs bedroom and Mrs Houk rushed upstairs, only to come back almost immediately, looking visibly shaken. 'Marilyn is dead – murdered in the most horrible manner,' she told her husband.

By the time the police arrived, followed by the coroner, it had been light for some time. After examining the body, the coroner, Dr Samuel Gerber, put the time of death as between 3.00 and 4.00 AM. 'The murder was committed with a blunt instrument,' he told the police. He hesitated, and then voiced his obvious disquiet. 'What worries me is the state of the room. It's in such a mindless disarray that it looks like some amateur attempt to make it appear as if the crime was committed while a robbery was taking place.' Looking around the room, Sergeant Robert Schottke, one of the best of Cleveland's homicide detectives, had to admit that Gerber had a point.

The police pretended to accept Sheppard's story, and then quietly began making their enquiries. One of the first things they dug up was that Sheppard had been having a torrid affair with Susan Hayes, who worked in the same office with him. Nor was it the only affair since Sheppard had married.

Suddenly, the clean-living, upright 'golden boy' had become ostracized by the society which he had served so well until the tragedy occurred. Unlike the titled or very rich in Britain, who tend to rally round when one of their members is in distress – as in the case of Lord Lucan – the wealthy burghers of Cleveland seemed to have turned against Sam Sheppard overnight. A whispering campaign was started up against him, and in this they were abetted by the local press, who launched an hysterical attack, culminating in the *Cleveland Press* demanding to know in thundering headlines why Sam Sheppard had not been arrested.

Although Sergeant Robert Schottke had been on the case from the beginning, and was already convinced that Sheppard was guilty of the murder of his wife, he would have liked more evidence before arresting him – especially as the flimsiest part of the case against Sheppard was the question of motive, which rested on nothing more than the fact that he had been unfaithful to his wife on a number of occasions. But by now the press had whipped up the fury of the public to such an extent that he had no option but to bow to public opinion and take Sheppard into custody.

Sam Sheppard was arrested and brought to trial on 18 October 1954. His arrival at the court-house was the usual circus that attended an American murder trial of this importance. Press flashbulbs blinked in rapid succession as Sheppard came out of the car and walked up the court-house steps, while the police struggled to control the enormous crowd that had gathered, mostly to throw abuse at the accused man. Inside the court-room it was almost as bad, with Judge Edwin Blythin having to pound his gavel to silence the hubbub before the trial could begin. Leading the prosecution was John Mahon, supported by Saul Danaceau and Thomas Parrino, who was to make something of a name for himself in this trial. Beside Sheppard sat William J. Corrigan, acting for his defence.

To sum up a trial which was one of the longest in American legal history, the case for the prosecution rested on a number of factors of a purely speculative nature which could not be supported by any concrete facts. Not that this deterred the prosecution. Accusations without much foundation were hurled by the prosecution across the courtroom, only to be contemptuously rejected by the defence. And so it went on, day after day, for over two months, leaving the jury exhausted but still convinced in their own minds that Sheppard was guilty as charged. Thanks to all the virulent attacks on him in the press, it was probably an opinion they had held from the moment they had sat down in the courtroom, and nothing that the defence could offer changed that opinion.

There were four things that had destroyed Sam Sheppard at that trial. One was the evidence of the coroner, Dr Gerber, who had stated categorically that a blood imprint found on a pillow beneath the dead woman's head had been made by a surgical instrument that Sheppard was likely to own. The fact that Dr Gerber could not say what sort of surgical instrument had been used, or that the instrument had never been found, was of little consequence to the jury, who seemed to think that Dr Gerber's evidence was highly significant.

The second concerned the fact that Sheppard was stripped to the waist when Mayor Houk and his wife had gone to the house. He had been unable to produce the shirt he had been wearing earlier on, and this, the prosecution contended, was because he had destroyed it as it was covered with blood stains.

Another piece of evidence against Sheppard was his wrist-watch which had been put into a canvas bag together with his fraternity ring and some keys before being thrown in the shrubbery. The watch face was speckled with blood. This was the only real piece of damning evidence produced by the prosecution, and it caused the defence deep concern as it seemed to prove beyond any reasonable doubt that it had got there while Sheppard was beating in his wife's head. There *was* another answer, but it took twelve years before Sheppard's lawyers came up with it.

Lastly, the enormous amount of hostility shown towards Sheppard had been fanned by the press and was prejudicial to his case before it had even come to court. In this climate of inexplicable hatred, it was almost inevitable that the jury should find him guilty. He was convicted of second-degree murder and sentenced to life imprisonment.

A month after the trial, Sheppard's grief-stricken mother committed suicide, and soon afterwards his father died of a broken heart. To add to the death toll, the murdered woman's father committed suicide, as did a member of the jury who had become so depressed after the trial that he had killed himself. In people's minds, Sheppard had been indirectly responsible for all their deaths.

After Sheppard had been sent to serve his life sentence in Ohio's Marion prison, the people of Cleveland went on with their lives very much as before, many of them smugly convinced that Sheppard had received no less than his just deserts. More than a dozen years were to pass before they were reminded of him again, and in such a way as to make some of them wonder if they had been right after all in condemning him so quickly.

During the intervening years there had been a number of attempts to secure a retrial at various levels, but without

success. Sheppard's hopes of getting one now seemed
hopeless – that is until Lee Bailey came on the scene. A
brilliant and flamboyant lawyer, who had the reputation
for pulling off spectacular coups in court in the manner of
the TV lawyer Perry Mason, he was just the sort of person
Sheppard needed to revitalize interest in his case, which
the media no longer considered newsworthy.

About the time that Bailey took over the case a young
and attractive German divorcee named Ariane came on
the scene. After reading of his case she had been
exchanging letters with Sheppard for some time. She
announced her intention of coming to the United States to
see him, a piece of news which Bailey greeted as a heaven-
sent opportunity to draw attention to his client, who was
fast becoming a forgotten man. The news of the divorcee's
impending arrival was leaked to the press, who were
waiting for her when she arrived at the prison and stepped
out of the taxi to face a barrage of exploding flashbulbs.
She turned out to be an extremely attractive young
woman and kept the photographers busier than ever as
she swept past and went through the gates into the prison.
Their meeting was something of a carefully orchestrated
farce, engineered by Bailey, with Sheppard and the
German woman exchanging love tokens while the guards
watched. It was one of those occasions that could happen
only in America.

From that point onwards, Bailey was never short of
publicity for his client – publicity moreover that had
swung round to being sympathetic towards Sheppard. By
the time he was eventually granted a retrial by the
Supreme Court, he was already married to the divorcee.
The new trial began on 24 October 1966, with Judge
Francis Talty presiding. This time Sheppard had a judge
who was well known for his fairness, and a brilliant
defence lawyer who could make the best of his case,
unhampered by all the prejudice that had made his
previous defence lawyer's task almost impossible. Acting

for the prosecution was John Corrigan (no relation to the Corrigan who had defended him in his previous trial and who had since died).

Although this trial was carried out in quite a different atmosphere to the previous one, there were still two particularly hostile witnesses. One was Sergeant Robert Schottke, who was still convinced that Sheppard was guilty, but even more serious was Dr Gerber. He had made something of a career for himself lecturing on the Sheppard case, which was invariably presented to his audience as one in which his 'evidence' had been so instrumental in putting Sheppard behind bars. Bailey took Gerber through his previous evidence point by point, and by the time he had finished the doctor's reputation was in shreds. First, he dealt with the blunt surgical instrument that Sheppard was supposed to have used to batter his wife to death.

'Was this blunt instrument ever found?' Bailey inquired.

Dr Gerber looked at him warily. 'No – it was never found.'

The glance that Bailey directed at the jury spoke volumes. The court stirred, and even Judge Talty seemed surprised.

Bailey did not pursue that matter further. Indeed, he did not need to: it was enough that Dr Gerber's evidence was now open to serious question. Anyway, Bailey had something that was even more interesting to place before the court.

'Is it not true that, even before the murder of Marilyn Sheppard, you were heard to say that one day you were going to "get" the Sheppards?' enquired Bailey blandly.

Dr Gerber flushed and hotly denied the allegation. But the damage had been done. At the previous trial his departure from the witness box was greeted with many nods of approval from those sitting in the courtroom. This time there were more than a few who watched him go with a look of disapproval on their faces.

Bailey had not finished yet. He called Sergeant Robert Schottke to the stand. Like Dr Gerber, his reputation had been enhanced since those days when he had testified against Sheppard, and he was now seen as a first-class officer by the local community. Bailey's brief but telling examination in the witness box did nothing to improve that reputation.

'You will remember the canvas bag which contained Dr Sheppard's watch and other items,' Bailey said.

'I do.'

'Did you at any time think of examining those items to see if you could find any fingerprints on them other than those belonging to Dr Sheppard?'

Schottke hesitated. 'No.'

Bailey then moved in for the kill. 'Then you did not find out just what prints were there before accusing the defendant of murder.'

'No.'

Seeing the case for the prosecution being steadily demolished under Bailey's cross-examination, Corrigan put on the stand the one witness whose evidence he considered was irrefutable. This was Dr Gerber's assistant, Mary Cowen, who had come to court armed with transparencies of the items found in the bag. Among them was Sheppard's wrist-watch. After putting her on the stand, Corrigan began to question her about some specks of blood found on the face of the watch.

'They were specks of flying blood,' Mary Cowen told him. 'They could only have got there while Dr Sheppard was battering his wife to death.'

'You are quite sure they could not have got there in any other way?'

'Quite sure,' was her firm reply.

This was the one piece of evidence that presented a serious problem for the defence. If Mary Cowen's statement was allowed to go uncontested it would nullify all the doubts that Bailey had cast on the previous evidence presented by the prosecution. He was convinced of Dr Sheppard's innocence, and until the prosecution had introduced the question of the 'flying blood', he had been certain that the jury was now on his side. Somehow he had to regain the ground he had just lost. But how?

When Bailey came up with the answer, it seemed so elementary that it was surprising no one had thought of it before. Examining the transparencies again he suddenly became aware that minute particles of blood were also on the *inside* of the watchstrap. This meant they could not have got there at the same time that Sheppard was supposed to have been murdering his wife.

When Bailey gave his final speech he was therefore able to say with confidence that the evidence was 'ten pounds of hog wash in a five pound bag'. The jury obviously agreed with him and brought in a verdict of not guilty, and the verdict of the first trial was overturned on the grounds that it was conducted in an atmosphere of 'prejudicial publicity'.

Sadly, Dr Sheppard's release after twelve years imprisonment was not to be the triumphant affair it should have been. When he tried to take up his medical work again, it was only to find that his patients treated him with suspicion, and that no insurance company would give him cover for being sued for negligence – a real danger for any medical man who has to deal with a public that has always seen litigation as a potential means of making money.

After having been forced to give up his profession, nothing seems to have gone right for Sheppard. Perhaps inevitably, in view of the unreal circumstances in which he and Ariane met, their marriage quickly foundered, and Sheppard found himself alone in the world again.

It was at this point that Sheppard's life took a strange and totally unexpected turn. He met an athlete named Strickland, married his nineteen-year-old daughter, and for a short time became a professional wrestler, before he was taken ill and died in 1970, a victim of the way in which society had treated him as much as the illness that had suddenly struck him down.

WHEN EAST MEETS WEST

Madame Fahmy

English murder case 1923

The great advocate Marshall Hall belonged to the old school of defence lawyers whose barnstorming performances belonged more to the Victorian theatre than to a court of law. Using all the old tricks of the trade, his performance began from the moment he sailed majestically into the court-room, making it clear to everyone that the star of the show had arrived. According to John Mortimer, in his introduction to the Penguin edition of *Famous Trials of Marshall Hall* by Edward Marjoribanks, published in 1950, his father had seen the great man in action and had often described Hall's first entry into court. Invariably he was preceded by three clerks ceremoniously carrying some of the props that he might need for his performance – a pile of handkerchiefs to blow into noisily when the prosecution was making a telling point against Hall's client, a carafe of water which he would knock over 'accidentally' when the accused was beginning to wilt under cross-examination, and an air cushion which he blew up to distract the attention of the jurors whenever the prosecution was making a key speech. An actor *manqué*, his resonant voice would fill the court-room as he pulled out all the stops to plead for his client's life, often using his arms outstreched in an imitation of the Scales of Justice, before bringing one down on the side representing his client's innocence. Whether these tricks made any difference to the outcome of any trial is debatable; certainly they made no difference to the judges, who had seen it all before.

If Hall manipulated jurors, it was not with the deliberate

intention of leading them into giving the wrong verdict, but rather to ensure that an innocent person was not punished for a crime they did not commit. If the occasional guilty client was declared innocent, far better that than someone should be unjustly hanged – as has happened more than once in Britain when the presumed infallibility of British justice was questioned and found wanting, too late to be of any help to the unfortunate soul whose body had long since been buried in an unmarked grave in the grounds of some prison.

Fortunately for his clients, Marshall Hall brought much more into a court-room than a bag of tricks. He had an incisive mind that had been honed to a razor-like sharpness through his many encounters in the court-room, which he always treated as a battlefield from which he was determined to emerge the victor, even when the case seemed hopeless. More often than not he succeeded. If there was the slightest flaw in the prosecution, he would see it immediately and turn it to his own advantage. His sympathy and understanding of human frailty gave him an insight into the character and personality of his client, which gave him the ability to defend them with a passionate sincerity that was lacking in most advocates and always impressed a jury. Little wonder that when Marshall Hall took on a case it was almost like a rubber stamp for an acquittal. At the time of his death in 1927, of the twenty-two people he had defended on murder charges only seven were found guilty without any exonerating circumstances.

His most personally satisfying triumph in court took place towards the end of his career, when he successfully defended Madame Fahmy when she was on trial for her life for the murder of her husband, Prince Fahmy Bey, a decadent Egyptian millionaire who had turned the life of his Parisian wife into a nightmare because of his unnatural sexual practices and cruel behaviour.

The case became a *cause célèbre*, mainly because it fired

the imagination of the general public with its echoes of a particular type of romantic fiction with an Oriental background, such as Robert Hichens's *The Garden of Allah* and Ethel Hull's *The Sheik*, made into a film starring Rudolph Valentino in 1921. More than any others of its kind, the latter story paralleled the case of the shooting of Prince Fahmy Bey, telling the tale of Diana Mayo, a proud English girl kidnapped by a sheik, whose brutal treatment of her finally won him her undying devotion. Any possible racial questions raised by indignant readers were put to rest when it was revealed that the sheik is the son of a well-heeled English peer.

All this may have made fun reading for some, but Fahmy Bey was not a hero in wolf's clothing like Hull's sheik, but an arrogant pervert whose unpleasant sexual tendencies would have discouraged any woman of a normal sexual appetite.

Madame Marguerite Laurent, as she was known before she married Fahmy Bey, already had one unfortunate marriage behind her – it ended when she was forced to divorce her husband for desertion. She was therefore a little wary and none too anxious to rush into marriage again when she first met Fahmy while he was working with the Egyptian Legation in Paris. At first she managed to keep him at arm's length, although he was charming and attentive and his behaviour all that a woman could wish for from someone who professed that he was madly in love with her. He bombarded her with ardent love letters and continued to be kind and considerate whenever they met, always giving the impression that he was a sophisticated man of the world who had liberated himself from the shackles of the rigid disciplines of the Moslem religion. When she went on holiday to Deauville, he pursued her and at last she gave in and became his mistress.

When he returned to Egypt, he wrote and asked her to join him and become his wife, saying, 'I see your head encircled by a crown, which I have reserved for you here. It is a crown I have reserved for you on your arrival in this beautiful country of my ancestors.' Unable to resist becoming the wife of an immensely rich prince whom she also happened to love, Madame Laurent set off for Egypt expecting to find *une vie de rêve*, as she wrote to a friend before leaving Paris. What she got instead was, as Sir Noel Coward's maid and cook delicately put it, a life of *toujours faire l'amour par la derrière*. It was not until her honeymoon that she became aware that Fahmy was a paederast, something he had been careful to conceal from her in Deauville.

Apart from this, his whole attitude towards her changed as soon as they were married. Instead of the charming and attentive lover she had come to know, he now treated her as a subservient creature who was expected to comply with his every wish.

By June 1923, Madame Fahmy's situation had become a desperate one. Trapped in an alien culture, she was never allowed out alone unless accompanied by her husband's male secretary, Said Enani, who watched her every movement and faithfully reported everything back to her husband. She struggled to maintain her sanity while Fahmy continued to hurl abuse at her and humiliate her at every conceivable opportunity – something which he saw as a necessity when having to deal with a Western woman whose spirit had still not been completely subjugated. An insight into his mind is given in a letter he wrote to Madame Fahmy's sister:

> ... Just now I am engaged in training her. Yesterday, to begin, I did not come down to lunch or dinner, and I also left her at the theatre. This will teach her, I hope, to respect my wishes. With women one must act with energy and be severe.

His actions sound more like those of a spoilt child trying to get his own back on his parents, rather than the behaviour of a grown man. Her hours away from him can only have come as a welcome relief. Far more serious were his frequent physical assaults for some alleged misdemeanour, such as the time she had dared to go to the cinema alone, when he had punched her in the face and dislocated her jaw.

Why did Madame Fahmy not try to free herself from this monster? Why did she not, for instance, simply obtain a divorce, as she had done with her previous husband? Because she was in no position to do so.

When she married Fahmy she elected to adopt the Moslem religion because an inheritance from his mother would be forfeited if he did not marry a woman of the faith. Madame Fahmy had laid down two stipulations at the time: she would not be forced to wear the veil and she would maintain the right to divorce her husband at any time if she so desired. Fahmy did not argue about the wearing of the veil, but when it came to signing the civil marriage contract, he flatly refused to allow the divorce condition to be inserted, by which time it was too late for Madame Fahmy to do anything about it.

In marrying Fahmy, his wife had forfeited a considerable allowance from her first husband. In exchange she would receive £2,000 from Fahmy as part of the marriage contract. In the event, Fahmy reneged yet again and all she ever received was £450 and an IOU 'from the richest man in Egypt', as Marshall Hall was careful to point out at the trial.

At the beginning of July 1923, Fahmy informed her that he was going to London and that she was to accompany him. When they arrived at the Savoy Hotel on 5 July, Madame Fahmy could look back on a marriage in which she had been degraded, beaten and abused. She could remember with even greater horror the occasion when, in one of his many displays of vile temper, her husband approached her with the Koran in his hand, swearing on it that one day he was going to kill her. All this was enough to make her kill him. The vital question was to arise whether or not she had shot him deliberately, or whether the shooting had been nothing more than an unfortunate accident.

On 10 July, the day before the shooting took place, London had sweltered in conditions of tropical heat. The sultry weather had persisted all day, and even the coming of the evening had done nothing to ease the almost intolerable conditions for those unused to this type of weather. At midnight the storm that had been impending all day began to move towards Central London, accompanied by crashes of thunder and vivid flashes of lightning that kept turning night into day as if a switch were being turned on and off by some demonic hand.

When the storm was at its height, the staff of the Savoy Hotel calmly carried on with their duties. One of them was a night porter named Beattie who had been a soldier in the First World War. He was wheeling some luggage along the corridor where Prince Fahmy and his party had their rooms when he heard three distinct explosions, each following the other in rapid succession. Thinking they sounded very much like revolver shots, Beattie ran to the room from where he thought the shots had come. He knocked at the door, and a few seconds later the door was flung open to reveal the distraught figure of Madame Fahmy standing in the doorway. Behind her he could see Prince Fahmy lying on the floor dressed in his pyjamas, with blood trickling from his mouth and a revolver lying on the bed. The night manager was hurriedly summoned and on seeing him Madame Fahmy cried out in French, 'What have I done? What will they do to me? Oh, sir, I have been married for six months, and I have suffered terribly.'

The English have always loved a murder case, and never more so than when it has occurred among the titled and wealthy. When the press reported the shooting of Prince Ali Kemel Fahmy Bey by his sultry-looking wife, the public seized it with its usual eagerness to know all the gory details. The murder lacked some of the more horrifying aspects of some of the cases that had been reported in the newspapers over the years, but the fascinating cast of players more than compensated. A decadent Egyptian prince, his European wife caught helplessly like a butterfly in a net of an inescapable situation, a sinister African servant straight out of the *Arabian Nights*, the Prince's male secretary (who was more than he seemed to be) and talk of obscene practices – what more could one ask from a murder which promised to become the trial of the decade? To cap it all, Marshall Hall, always reliable for an entertaining performance in court, was to act for the defendant.

The trial of Madame Fahmy opened in London's Central Criminal Court on 10 September 1923, with Mr Percival Clarke and Mr Eustace Fulton appearing for the Crown before Mr Justice Rigby Smith. Marshall Hall, who had accepted the brief for the defence for 652 guineas, was supported by Sir Henry Curtis Brown and Mr Roland Oliver. When Marshall Hall and his team entered the court that day, they all knew that once more the famous advocate was about to defend a client whose chances of acquittal were remote.

In his opening speech for the Crown, Percival Clarke spelt out Madame Fahmy's position all too clearly to the jury in simple terms which Marshall Hall might well have used himself if he had been appearing for the prosecution. 'Every homicide is presumed to be murder unless the contrary is shown. From her own lips it is known that she caused the death of her husband. And in the absence of any other offence, you must find her guilty of murder.'

Marshall Hall and his team had to prove, therefore, that there was another 'offence' and, not only that, also had to win the sympathy of the jury by establishing that Prince Fahmy was the sadistic pervert that his wife was to claim he had been – no easy task when all the witnesses to

Fahmy's behaviour were loyal members of his staff. That
their loyalty to Prince Fahmy came first was made clearly
evident when Marshall Hall began questioning the secretary, Said Enani. The following exchange between the two
men is indicative of the formidable task that lay ahead for
Marshall Hall.

'Do you know that he swore on the Koran to kill her?'

'No.'

'Did you know that she was in fear of her life?'

'No. I never knew.'

'Was not the Madame Fahmy of 1922 a totally different
person from the Madame Fahmy of 1923?'

Enani shrugged. 'Perhaps.'

'From being a gay, cheerful, entertaining and fascinating woman, did she not become sad, broken and miserable?'

Said Enani avoided the question. 'They were always
quarrelling.'

On further questioning, he also claimed no knowledge
of the incident that had occurred in Paris when Fahmy
had seized his wife by the throat and tried to strangle her.
The only statement of any significance that Marshall Hall
was able to wring out of him was his agreement that
Prince Fahmy had reneged on his promise to allow his
wife to insert the clause in the marriage contract allowing
her to divorce him.

'After the religious ceremony, then, he could divorce
her, as she was a Moslem, but she could not divorce him,
even if he chose to take three wives?'

'That is so,' Said Enani agreed.

Marshall Hall also put to him that his master had been a
man of vicious and perverted sexual appetite, which Said
Enani vigorously denied. Hall was on delicate ground here
as it had been rumoured that Said Enani himself had been
one of the Prince's many homosexual lovers, and he had
no wish to enter an area strewn with minefields where an
ill-considered remark could have blown up in his face and

ove: Emily Kaye,
rdered by Patrick Mahon
Hulton Deutsch Collection)

Above: Patrick Mahon with
his daughter
(© *Hulton Deutsch Collection*)

Below left: Madame Marie Fahmy Bey, tried for the murder of her husband (© *Hulton Deutsch Collection*)

Above right: Madame Fahmy after her acquittal, when she became an actress (© *Hulton Deusch Collection*)

Above: Gay Gibson (© *Popperfoto*)

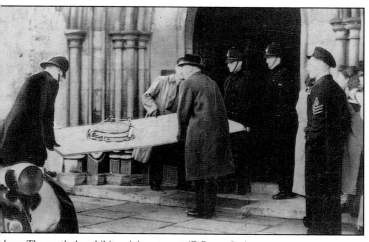

Above: The porthole exhibit arriving at court (© *Popperfoto*)

Above: Tony Mancini
(© *Hulton Deutsch Collection*)

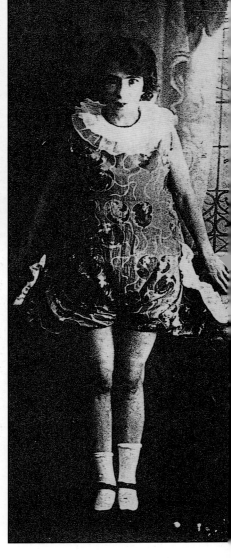

Right: Violette Kaye, his victim, pictured in costume for a production of *Dick Whittington* c.1920
(© *Hulton Deutsch Collection*)

Above: The trunk in Mancini's bedroom (© *Hulton Deutsch Collection*)

Right: Alfred Arthur Rouse
(© *Syndication International*)

Below: The burnt-out car in
the Rouse murder case
(© *Syndication International*)

Above: Juliet Hulme and Pauline Parker after being remanded in Christchurch, New Zealand (© *Popperfoto*)

Above: Alma Rattenbury seen entering a London nursing home after her acquittal (© *Hulton Deutsch Collection*)

Above: The police forcing the crowd away from the Old Bailey after the result of the Rattenbury trial (© *Hulton Deutsch Collection*)

lowered the high regard in which he was held. By leaving
the character of the witness intact he made it clear that
both sides should have an unspoken gentleman's agreement that no witness or the defendant should be point-
lessly attacked merely to score some points that were of
little value to either the prosecution or the defence. In this,
both Percival Clarke and Eustace Fulton showed admir-
able restraint, never once indulging in any court-room
histrionics that might sway a jury into giving an unfair
verdict.

Marshall Hall was on firmer ground when he cross-
examined Madame Fahmy. She spoke only halting
English, and certainly not enough to understand what was
going on in court. But Marshall Hall had been fortunate
enough to secure the services of an attractive young
French woman named Odette Simon, and it was through
her that he addressed a series of questions to Madame
Fahmy, whose answers were to gain her the sympathy of
the jury.

First he guided her through the salient details of her
unhappy life with Fahmy Bey, even getting her to list the
minor humiliations she had suffered when he had put her
under constant surveillance by six Africans who took it in
turn to watch her every second of the day. One of them
had been an enormous man named Costa, who had
followed her everywhere, even accompanying her into the
bedroom when she wanted to change her dress. When she
had complained to her husband, he had merely shrugged
and said, 'It is his right.'

As the catalogue of Fahmy's acts of ill treatment and
violence towards his wife mounted, Marshall Hall sensed
that the jury were now sympathetic towards his client. As
the court-room listened enthralled and more than a little
shocked by the story being unfolded by Madame Fahmy,
he moved on to the events that had led up to the shooting.

On that night Fahmy offered his wife a wad of money
to pay for an operation she needed for haemorrhoids, on

the condition that she submitted to his will. She refused, a violent row had ensued and with more spirit than usual, Madam Fahmy had threatened to smash a bottle over his head. Later the couple had gone down to dinner and were in the middle of their meal when the leader of the orchestra approached them and asked Madame Fahmy if there was any particular piece of music she would like to hear.

'Thank you very much,' Madame Fahmy said, 'but my husband is going to kill me in the next twenty-four hours, and I am not anxious for music.'

The orchestra leader took her odd reply in his stride, as one might expect from one of the Savoy's employees. 'I hope you will be with us tomorrow,' he said gravely as he retreated.

Afterwards, Madame Fahmy and her husband went upstairs, where yet another violent row flared up in the passageway outside their room. Suddenly, without any warning, Fahmy had seized her by the throat saying, 'I will kill you. I will kill you.' Now frightened out of her wits, Madame Fahmy had broken free from his stranglehold and had run into the bedroom and picked up the gun she always kept to hand to guard her jewellery. When Fahmy followed her into the room, she fired a shot through the window to frighten him. Undeterred by the sight of the gun, Fahmy was about to spring on her, when she turned her head to one side and fired several shots blindly in his direction.

When she had finished her testimony, Marshall Hall turned to the jury. 'I submit that this poor wretch of a woman,' he said emotionally, 'suffering the tortures of the damned, driven to desperation by the brutality and beastliness of the man whose will she dared to oppose, thought that he was carrying out the threat he had constantly made, and that when he seized her by the neck, he was indeed about to kill her.'

Marshall Hall then cross-examined Robert Churchill, a

gunsmith and an acknowledged expert on small arms. The gun that had been used was a .32 Browning automatic that had to be pulled for each shot and needed a fairly strong finger on the trigger to pull it. This seemed to imply that each shot had been deliberately pumped into Fahmy, rather than let loose by a frightened woman involuntarily firing. Knowing that left unchallenged it could prove dangerous to his client's case, Marshall Hall pressed Churchill hard on this point and Churchill eventually conceded that if the gun had been tightly gripped, only a very small pressure was needed to fire off each shot.

By the fourth day of the trial Marshall Hall must have known that he was well on the way to acquiring an acquittal for Madame Fahmy when he rose to make the final speech for the defence.

'This woman,' he began 'made one great mistake – she married an Oriental. It is common knowledge that the Oriental's treatment of women does not fit in with the way the Western woman considers she should be treated by her husband. Why was this woman afraid? The cause of this case is the atmosphere which we cannot understand – the Eastern feeling of possession of women, the Turk in his harem – this is something almost unintelligible to us, something we cannot deal with . . .'

In this manner Marshall Hall began what was probably the most dramatic speech of his career. It was also one that was loaded with racial prejudice and would have caused an uproar if it had been uttered in court today.

The racism was even more apparent the next day when Marshall Hall dealt with the events that led up to the killing of Fahmy Bey. He referred to the storm and the effects that it must have had on a woman of a nervous temperament. 'Imagine its effect on a woman who had been outraged, beaten, abused, degraded. Now her degrader was advancing menacingly on her.' At this point he imitated what he imagined was the crouch of a stealthily advancing Oriental. 'In her desperation – as he crouched for the last time like an animal, like an Oriental, she turned the pistol to his face, and to her horror the thing went off.' He held up the pistol which he let fall to the floor as he described how Fahmy had fallen dead to the ground. It must have been a performance that might have been effective enough when Sir Henry Irving trod the boards at the Lyceum, but today might only have raised a giggle. But on that day in the court-room, the effect was electrifying.

Finally, he recalled a scene from Robert Hichen's novel *Bella Donna*, another popular desert romance of the time. 'You will remember the final scene when the woman goes out of the gates of the garden into the dark night of the desert. I want you to open the gates so that this Western woman can go out, not into the dark night of the desert, but back to her friends, who love her in spite of her weaknesses. You will open the gate and let this woman go back into the light of God's great Western sun.' Dripping with sweat, he turned to Percival Clarke. 'To use the words of my learned friend's great father in a case in which I heard him many years ago at the Old Bailey, "I don't ask you for a verdict, I demand it at your hands."'

Who could refuse such an appeal from this old war horse of the court? Certainly not the jury who had sat riveted by Marshall Hall's performance. They returned with their verdict within the hour – not guilty of murder, and not guilty of manslaughter. Their verdict was greeted with loud cheers from the court.

Instead of being criticized for the racist tones of his final speech, Marshall Hall won the approval of some of the press for drawing attention to the inadvisability of marrying an Oriental in the belief that such unions were romantic. 'They are not romantic,' the *Daily Mirror* said sternly. 'They are ridiculous, and the sensational revelations of the trial which terminated on Saturday will not be without their use if they bring home that fact to the sentimental naive girl.'

The single note of criticism came from the Egyptian Bar, which sent a long cable to the British Attorney General protesting at Marshall Hall's attack on Egyptians and, indeed, the whole East. Hall seemed genuinely surprised to learn that he had gone too far, and wrote to express his apology for causing offence where none had been intended. The affair blew over and he went on to appear in several more cases before his death in 1927. He was the last of his kind and even after all these years his reputation lingers on, despite that one lapse when he allowed his love of the theatrical to override other considerations.

As for Madame Fahmy, after writing to Marshall Hall expressing her gratitude for defending her so ably, she continued to correspond with him for some time before she disappeared from sight, though she is known to have been living in Paris during the Second World War.

A NASTY SMELL IN THE HOUSE

Frederick Deeming

Australian murder case 1892

M r Stafford was in a happy mood, and for a very good reason. After all the months of waiting he thought he had finally found a tenant for his house in Andrew Street in Windsor, a suburb of Melbourne, the city which seemed to have suffered most in the economic depression that raged across Australia in the 1890s, causing mass unemployment and widespread misery. Although Mr Stafford was not suffering as much as some people, he had bought the house in Andrew Street as an investment in the late 1880s when there had been a tremendous boom in the property market. The investment had now gone sour on him, and the house had remained empty ever since it had been vacated by a Mr Druin, an Englishman with a Liverpool accent who had left rather suddenly.

His potential tenant was a single woman, and Mr Stafford was showing her around the house which, to his relief, she seemed to like. That was till she suddenly became aware of an unpleasant smell coming from one of the bedrooms. As she stood there, wrinkling her nose with distaste, Mr Stafford's heart sank. After she had fled, saying that the house was not for her, Mr Stafford went to see his letting agent, who immediately offered to return to the house with him.

They sniffed around the bedroom. The smell seemed to come from beneath the hearthstone. As soon as they began to prise it up, the whole room was filled with an overpowering stench that sent them, gagging, to the window.

Although there was a layer of cement under the hearthstone, both Mr Stafford and the estate agent knew that the terrible smell came from a decomposed corpse. They summoned the police, and in due course they arrived and dug up the remains of a woman whose skull had obviously been fractured by a heavy instrument. Thus began a long trail of horror that led to Perth, Sydney, across the ocean to Liverpool and back again to Australia before the world knew the full extent of the horrendous crimes of Frederick Deeming, a man with a cold-blooded taste for murder, rather than financial gain or any other logical motive.

The most cunning murderer often makes one fatal, careless mistake that is enough to bring him to the gallows or life imprisonment. In Deeming's case it was a torn luggage ticket for two which had been thrown carelessly into the grate. The ticket had been issued by the shipping offices of *Kaiser Wilhelm II*, travelling from Melbourne to Sydney, to Albert Williams – just one of the many aliases used by Frederick Deeming. Convinced he was the man they were looking for, the police issued a warrant for his immediate arrest.

About the same time as the body was discovered, a nineteen-year-old girl named Kate Rounsefell was on her way from Bathurst to meet a Baron Swanston, the man she had decided to marry. She had met him on board a ship travelling from Adelaide to Sydney, and had been completely captivated by his charming manner. She had stayed the night in Sydney before going to see her elder sister in Bathurst, some sixty miles away. The baron had spent the night in the same hotel, and the next day had taken her on a tour of the city. To her amazement, the baron had suddenly proposed to her.

'I must speak to my sister first,' she said.

'Let me come with you.' The baron gave her a winning smile. 'It's only right your sister should see the man you are to marry.'

On meeting Baron Swanston, Kate's sister had also been impressed. 'It's all rather sudden,' she said to her sister when they were alone, 'but I have the feeling that he would make a good husband.'

'And rather a wealthy one, I would imagine,' Kate said.

On arriving in Melbourne at the hotel where she had arranged to meet her future husband, she found a telegram from her sister. It read: 'For God's sake go no further!' Mystified, she went out to buy a newspaper and found the familiar face of Baron Swanston staring at her from the front page. On reading the caption under the picture she practically fainted on the spot. Baron Swanston, as she knew him, was wanted for the murder of his wife. Only the man mentioned in the caption was not Swanston, but Albert Williams.

If the body had not been discovered at that time, and Deeming's picture printed in the newspapers, there is little doubt that Kate Rounsefell would also have been murdered by Deeming in the course of time. It is said that as a result of the terrible shock she received, her hair turned white. At least she learned a lesson that applies as much today as it did then – never trust a complete stranger.

After the discovery of the body the police found another vital clue. Amid the litter in the backyard they came across a crumpled-up invitation card for a dinner that Williams had held at the Commercial Hotel in Rainhill, a small village outside Liverpool in England. The Australian police immediately sent a cable to the Rainhill police, asking for their help in tracing him. At the same time the *Melbourne Argus* cabled their representative in London, asking him to go to Rainhill as quickly as possible to find out what he could. Between them they unearthed a disturbing story.

Travelling under the name of Williams, Deeming had arrived in Rainhill, describing himself as an Inspector of Regiments who had come to the village to rent a house for his employer, Colonel Brooks. After making some enquiries, he had learned that a Mrs Mather owned an available property called Dinham Villa. He rented it on the Colonel's behalf and then settled in at the Commercial Hotel to await the arrival of his employer. During his brief stay in the village he had met Mrs Mather's daughter, Emily, whom he had married after a whirlwind courtship. After the marriage, he had thrown a farewell party at the hotel before setting off unexpectedly for Australia with his new bride, leaving a mountain of unpaid bills behind him. Colonel Brooks, of course, had still not put in an appearance.

There was also some talk of an unknown woman who had suddenly arrived in the village, accompanied by four young children. Claiming that the woman was his married sister, Deeming had installed the family in Dinham Villa, saying that they would only be staying there for a very short while. The family left as suddenly as they had arrived, their departure unnoticed by anyone.

As soon as the family was gone, Deeming had asked Mrs Mather's permission to cement the floor in one of the rooms, as it was in too bad a condition for Colonel Brooks to lay down his expensive Oriental carpets. Permission was granted, and Deeming had entered the house with a large bag of cement, a pickaxe and a trowel, and had remained there for the best part of the day before emerging in obvious high spirits.

On hearing this, the police descended in force on Dinham Villa, armed with shovels and pickaxes. The moment they entered the house they were assailed by a dreadful smell, similar to the one that had greeted the Australian police when they entered the house in Windsor. Here the police discovered the body of a woman and four young children. Who were they, and why had they been murdered?

This was not as difficult to find out as might be imagined. The police knew that Deeming originally came from Liverpool, and they had no trouble in finding the family home, where his two brothers still lived. They were

shown the corpses and they identified them as being
Deeming's first wife, Marie James, and her four children
by Deeming, whom he had callously deserted in Sydney,
leaving their mother so destitute that she had been forced
to scrape a living of sorts by singing in the streets of the
city. Somehow she had managed to make her way back to
the family home in Liverpool, only to be told that
Deeming was no longer there. Unfortunately for her,
Deeming had told his brothers that he would be staying at
Rainhill, and she had gone there, determined to claim her
rights.

One can imagine Deeming's dismay at seeing her and
the children, and one can imagine, too, his inward fury at
the thought of having to give up Emily Mather, whom he
was already planning to marry. We shall never know what
he said to his wife when he faced her that day at Rainhill.
What we do know is that he took her and the children to
Dinham Villa, where he allowed them to stay alive just
long enough to establish that it was his 'sister' and her
family who were paying him a visit. Then he slaughtered
them, cutting the throats of his wife and three of the
children, and strangling the fourth, his nine-year-old
daughter.

While investigations were uncovering this black tale,
Deeming had been spotted and arrested at Southern
Cross, a mining community some 250 miles from Perth.
Roughly coinciding with this period of time, Deeming's
true identity had been established. Born in Liverpool, he
had started his career of crime as a confidence trickster
who had worked and lived around the city for a number of
years, during which time he had married. His career in
England had ended abruptly after he had murdered his
first wife, Marie James, and left for Australia with his
second wife, Emily. He arrived in Sydney in 1891, and
worked there as a plumber and gas fitter until 1892, when
his second wife shared the same fate as the first.

When all this came out in the press, feelings against

Deeming ran high, with both countries wanting to see him dangling at the end of the hangman's noose. As it was, Deeming was lucky to reach the court-room alive. When he left Perth on the long train journey to Albany in order to make the sea voyage to Melbourne, hundreds of people were waiting for him at every whistle stop and station. On one occasion, the mob nearly managed to get on the train, which could have led to Deeming being lynched on the spot.

Throughout most of the journey, Deeming sat silent and seemingly impervious to all the catcalls and jeers that greeted him along the way, though occasionally he smiled at the crowds as if he were royalty acknowledging the cheers of his subjects. Seldom had a murderer going to an almost inevitable appointment with the hangman appeared so calm and relaxed as Deeming on that journey, which must have seemed interminable to those who were escorting him to Melbourne. No sooner were they past one station than another screaming mob awaited them at the next, where yet another fusillade of bricks and stones were hurled at the passing train. Apart from a handful of liberal-minded people who believed that Deeming should go through the due processes of the law before being executed, practically everyone in the state would gladly have lynched Deeming on the spot if they could have got their hands on him, such was popular hatred at that time.

The popular press, never noted for its sober approach to a sensational murder case, had a field day when writing of Deeming's progress across the country. If they did not go so far as actually inciting a public lynching, they were not far short of it. With this seething hatred, Deeming was lucky to have reached the ship taking him to Melbourne, let alone the safety of a prison cell.

Once he had been smuggled aboard the SS *Ballarat*, bound for Melbourne, the voyage passed without incident, though taking Deeming around the deck was something of a nightmare for Deeming's escort, faced with the task of fending off hostile passengers who would have gladly thrown Deeming overboard given half a chance. As for Deeming, he still seemed quite indifferent to the hostility of everyone on board, including the seamen, who taunted him openly in defiance of their officers who issued orders to ignore him.

The real trouble did not begin until they reached Melbourne. When Deeming stepped out on to the deck in the company of his escort on the morning of Friday 1 April 1892, they were to be greeted by the incredible sight of thousands of people gathered on the foreshore of Port Phillip Bay, where they had been waiting since the early hours to catch a glimpse of the monster whose murderous activities had outraged a whole nation. As he stood there, listening to the sound of jeering voices floating across the waters, Deeming's customary composure deserted him and he turned, panic-stricken, to Detective Sergeant Cawsey who was at his side.

'Don't worry,' Cawsey said curtly. 'We'll get you to the prison safely.'

A cutter was sent out in one direction, while Deeming and his escort slipped quietly away in the direction of St Kilda pier. They arrived there just in time to bundle Deeming into a waiting police wagon before the crowds realized what was happening, and came streaming down to the jetty. His arrival in the city was greeted by more sensational headlines and vitriolic articles, all of them echoing the earlier comment of the *Melbourne Argus*: 'The public will gladly witness the wretch's dying struggle.'

By the time that Deeming went on trial on 28 April, his solicitor had managed to find him one of the best defence lawyers in the country. This was Alfred Deakin, a brilliant advocate who was to become Prime Minister of Australia three times. Deakin was faced with an impossible task where the best he could hope for was a verdict of guilty but insane. To make matters worse, the legal definition of insanity in those days was very different from what it is now – the defence had to prove to the court's satisfaction that his client was unaware that he was doing wrong when he committed the crime. This was so obviously not the case with Deeming that it seems surprising that Deakin even bothered to try to persuade the court otherwise, a view that was obviously shared by Mr Justice Hodges, who listened impatiently to the opinions of the medical men Deakin put on the stand before dismissing their evidence out of hand. Reading the reports of the trial one gets the distinct impression that Mr Justice Hodges shared the general view that little time should be wasted in sending Deeming to the gallows.

Deakin continued to do his best. Time and time again he tried to prove that his client was insane, only to be brought to a halt by some tart comment from the judge, who was becoming extremely annoyed with Deakin's relentless attempts to prove Deeming insane. On the third day Deeming entered the stand and made a long rambling speech which was faithfully reported by the newspapers.

'I have not had a fair trial,' Deeming told the court. 'It is not the law which is trying me, but the press. The case was prejudiced even before my arrival by the exhibitions of photographs in shop windows, and it is by this means that I was identified ... If I could believe that I committed the murders I would plead guilty rather than submit to the gaze of the people in this court – the ugliest race of people I have ever seen ...'

As can be imagined, that last remark did nothing to endear Deeming to those in the court-room.

Afterwards he stated that he suffered from loss of memory and could not remember any incident which would have led him to committing the crimes of which he was accused. He rounded off a speech that had lasted for nearly an hour by saying, 'I do not hesitate to give up my life. It would be a pleasure. I have fought the blacks on the Zambesi and have fought lions single-handed. What is life to a man like me, whose prospects the newspapers and the public have ruined for ever? I do not expect justice ...'

The next day Alfred Deakin rose to make his final speech for the defence, which lasted for two hours. He first attacked the press for launching a campaign of hate which had fallen just short of openly advocating lynch law, and then told the court that the evidence was purely circumstantial, and that the prosecution had not brought forward a single witness who had seen any of the murders committed.

There is no doubt that Deakin did his best for his client, though he perhaps rather confused the issue by drawing attention to the evidence of some of the medical men who had examined Deeming, and had expressed doubts as to his sanity. Either the evidence had been purely circumstantial, or Deeming was guilty but insane. As it happened, Deakin's attempt to ride two horses at once made little difference to the judge and jury, who had been convinced of Deeming's guilt before he had even stepped into the court-room, and wanted to see him hanged as soon as possible.

The jury paid lip service to justice by being out for more than an hour before they returned with their verdict – guilty, and not insane. After the judge had passed the death sentence on him, Deeming thanked the judge politely and sauntered down to his cell, his hands in his pockets.

During the days that led up to his execution, which had been set for 22 May 1892, Deeming's air of self-assurance gradually slipped away. He now dreaded death and threatened to commit suicide rather than face the executioner. When the day for him to die did finally arrive, he walked into the execution shed bravely enough, taking a few last drags at one of his cigars before he was led over to the hangman's noose by the executioner and his assistant, both wearing false beards. A group of sombre-faced men in black frock coats watched while Deeming was pinioned

and a hood placed over his head. Unlike most executions
in which the victim is dealt with as swiftly and as merci-
fully as possible, Deeming's execution was a long drawn-
out affair, and he was forced to stand on the trap-door
while the prison chaplain droned through the whole of the
burial service. When at last it was over, Deeming just had
time to say 'May the Lord receive my spirit,' before the
trap-door opened and he plunged to his death. When the
news that justice had been done was broadcast, a great
cheer went up from the thousands waiting outside.

Much was written about Deeming, both before and
immediately after his death – it was even falsely claimed
that he was Jack the Ripper, whose murderous activities in
Whitechapel had ceased only a few years earlier. But what
explains his cold-blooded behaviour? Anyone trying to
write a true account of Deeming's life before he had
murdered his two wives has the difficult task of sorting out
the facts from the fiction he had woven around himself.

Born in 1842 into a family with a history of insanity, he
was the son of a tinsmith who had ended his days in a
lunatic asylum after having made four attempts to cut his
throat. As a boy Deeming was known to his friends as
'Mad Fred' and he was supported by his family until he
was eighteen, when he became a ship's steward. When he
returned to Liverpool several years later, it was to inform
everyone that he had been working in the gold fields of
South Africa. After his mother died in 1875, Deeming
was inconsolable for a long time before he eventually
rallied his spirits and went back to sea again. After visiting
Calcutta he had a severe attack of brain fever which left
him subject to delusions in which he began to believe he
was able to see the spirit of his mother. It was about this
time, one suspects, that he became dangerous, rather than
a man who merely suffered from the delusion that he was
a man of importance.

1890 saw him in Antwerp, posing as Lord Dunn. Even
allowing for all his petty embezzlements, his capacity for

raising money to support himself is to be marvelled at. What was there about him, one wonders, that made him so attractive to women and made people so ready to part with their cash? He was a very tall but unattractive man with cold eyes and a hard face, and who normally sported a straggling moustache that did nothing for his general appearance.

His return to Liverpool must have been something of an anti-climax. He was still remembered by many, who were not impressed by his newly found grand manner. Perhaps it was the hostility of those who knew him in Liverpool that made him go to Rainhill, where he was unknown. His decision to do so was something that the people of the village were to greatly regret – not least the mother of Emily Mather, whom he murdered in Australia.

There is not the slightest doubt that Deeming was insane. What is surprising is that for much of the time he was considered by so many people as being merely eccentric and somewhat odd. But then the English have always had a soft spot for their eccentrics.

CHARMLESS CHARLOTTE

Charlotte Bryant

English murder case 1935

No one in their right mind would have called Charlotte Bryant an attractive woman. It would have been more appropriate to refer to her as a slightly retarded illiterate, or a drunken lice-ridden slut who looked much older than her true age. She was thirty-three years old when she stood in the dock of the Dorchester Assizes on the charge of murdering her husband, and a more unlikely sex object it would be difficult to find anywhere. The jury and the public in the court must have been shocked, therefore, to learn that her sexual favours had been much in demand among the menfolk of the little Dorset village of Over Compton, near Yeovil.

The sad thing with Charlotte was that she had started off as a reasonably attractive young woman. What had turned her into a sad travesty of womanhood was grinding poverty, gradually dragging herself and her husband down until they were living in conditions that rivalled those portrayed by Gustave Doré in his drawings depicting the appalling living conditions of the Victorian poor.

Irish by birth, she was living in Londonderry in 1922 when she first met her husband, Frederick Bryant, who was serving with the infamous Black and Tans, whose brutal and repressive treatment of the Irish made them the most feared of all the English troops stationed there. Before she met him she had slept with a large number of the soldiers stationed in the local barracks. Unlike most of the troops, who were sensible enough to treat their sexual encounters as nothing more than a pleasant diversion from their boring and often unpleasant existence among a hostile community, Frederick took his relationship seriously enough to want to marry her. When his tour of duty was over he took Charlotte with him back to England, and they were married in Somerset.

Their downward spiral into abject poverty began when he left the Army and took a job as a labourer in Over Compton, a village lacking the social amenities that Charlotte was hoping to enjoy in England. It was all very much of a let-down. Charlotte had hoped that by going to England she would enjoy a better standard of living than the one she had been used to in Ireland. Even her husband had proved to be something of a disappointment. When she had first met him he had presented an attractive if somewhat sinister figure in his Black and Tan uniform. Now he was a humble farm worker, coming home with his boots caked with mud, he was no longer the dashing figure he had once seemed.

As time went by, their already straitened circumstances became worse and they were forced to move to Coombe, a more inaccessible village without even a bus service to somewhere like Taunton which she had been able to visit while they were in Over Compton. Boredom, and the sheer necessity of making some extra money to make ends meet, made her turn to part-time prostitution, especially as she had always enjoyed sex for its own sake.

Whatever looks Charlotte might have had began to deteriorate rapidly but, unaccountably, she was not lacking in clients, or the occasional lover (who meant little more to her than her paying customers). By then, Frederick was past caring what she did. As he commented bitterly to one of his acquaintances who had informed him that Charlotte was selling her body, 'I don't care what she does. Four pounds a week is better than thirty shillings.'

Their squalid existence was not helped by the couple's careless disregard for any safety measure in their own sex life, which seems to have thrived despite Frederick's awareness of Charlotte's part-time prostitution. Over the

years five children were born, which meant extra mouths
that had to be fed.

Unlike some prostitutes, who are supposed to despise
men, Charlotte's head was full of romantic dreams of
meeting a man who would make her happy. When
Leonard Parsons came on the scene, he must have seemed
to her to be the very embodiment of those dreams. A
good-looking and well-built gypsy vagrant with a shock of
black hair and blue eyes, he must have seemed to Charlotte the very answer to her prayers.

She met Parsons casually just before Christmas 1933,
and immediately fell in love with him and, without bothering to consult her husband, invited him to have
Christmas dinner with them. Parsons was in rooms in the
village at the time, and the one thing he had been
dreading was spending Christmas Day alone, staring at the
walls. Charlotte's invitation was therefore more than
welcome.

On Christmas Day he presented himself at the Bryant's
house, where he received an unexpectedly warm welcome
from Frederick, who was glad to have some male
company. The two men got on so well together that
Frederick suggested that he should stay with them until he
was ready to go on his way again. Parsons gladly accepted
the offer and moved in, thereby starting off a train of
events which were to lead to Frederick's murder and
Charlotte being put on trial for her life.

To start with, everything went smoothly, especially for
Charlotte and Parsons, who became lovers almost
immediately. Even Frederick seemed perfectly happy with
having Parsons in the house. For some strange reason it
never seems to have occurred to him that his wife might
be going to bed with Parsons as soon as he was out of the
house.

Instead, he and Parsons became bosom pals. Frederick
would come home at the end of the day to find Parsons
there with more tales of life on the road, selling trashy

goods from door-to-door. Charlotte, meanwhile, sat quietly, only half listening to them while she dreamed of a life with Parsons.

When Frederick eventually found out what was going on under his own roof he was shocked and angry. Despite his acceptance of the way that Charlotte earned her money, he had no intention of tolerating Charlotte conducting a clandestine affair in his own home. Parsons was ordered to leave the house and Charlotte went off to sulk in another room. Convinced that without Parsons her life would be even more intolerable than it was already, she packed her bags and left the next day, taking two of the children with her. Two days later she came back to her husband, who forgave her.

If Bryant thought that he had seen the last of Parsons, he was sadly mistaken. Charlotte had hardly settled back in the house than she received a telegram from Parsons asking her to meet him. In all fairness to Charlotte, she did not go behind her husband's back and meet Parsons. Instead, she showed the telegram to Bryant, who told her grimly to keep the appointment, but that he would be coming along too. The meeting took place at Bradford Hollow, near Babylon Hill, where Bryant told Parsons to keep away from his wife, while Charlotte stood quietly at his side, rather enjoying the situation of having two men fighting over her. Somewhere amid the wrangling, the course of conversation changed, and Bryant found himself discussing the possibility of Parsons returning to the cottage. Bryant weakly gave in, and in due course Parsons resumed his old status in the Bryant household.

This strange and grubby ménage à trois was one that was doomed from the start. Why Bryant ever agreed to it is something of a mystery. It has been suggested that he had become sexually inadequate, and saw Parsons's presence in the house as a welcome escape from Charlotte's demands. Whatever the reason, there must have been times when he felt miserable and humiliated when he heard Charlotte noisily performing in bed with Parsons.

Charlotte's attitude towards Parsons remained unchanged. Only too conscious that whatever looks she might have had were completely gone, she became extremely possessive – something that irritated Parsons, who was a wanderer by nature, and moreover, already had ties with a common-law wife and four children of his own – facts of which Charlotte was fully aware but chose to ignore.

When Charlotte began talking of leaving her husband and going off with him, Parsons's ardour began to cool rapidly, and Charlotte realized that something had to be done – and quickly.

Soon afterwards, Bryant was taken ill with violent stomach pains after one lunch-time. This was hardly surprising as Charlotte had laced his food with arsenic. The local physician, Dr McCarthy, was summoned, but did not arrive until the early evening, when he found Bryant suffering from cramp in his legs. He diagnosed gastroenteritis. Bryant soon recovered and went back to work, only to go down with a second bout with the same symptoms. By this time Parsons had become bored with the whole domestic situation and had decided to leave, telling Charlotte that he was seeking his luck elsewhere.

Charlotte watched in despair as he left the house. Bryant had stubbornly refused to succumb to the arsenic she had been feeding him, and as a result of her failure to poison him she was in danger of losing the man she loved. Like so many people at the end of an affair – even a squalid one like this – she could not accept that it was over. Instead, she began making plans to get Parsons back. The first thing on the agenda was to make sure that her husband did not recover from the third attack of 'gastro-enteritis' that he was about to have at any moment.

The attack came the next day and was so severe that Dr McCarthy became extremely worried about his patient. He left, after putting Bryant on a special diet ignored by

Charlotte. While Bryant was struggling to keep alive,
Charlotte left him for the day to manage as best he could
while she went by private car to Weston-super-Mare,
where she had heard Parsons was living in a gypsy
encampment outside the town. On her arrival she was met
by Priscilla Loveridge, the woman Parsons was living with.
Her mother, who seems to have been the archetypal pipe-
smoking gypsy woman, was with her. Parsons was conveniently elsewhere. The two women were amicable
enough, but they made it quite clear to Charlotte before
she left that there was no chance of Parsons ever coming
back.

On Saturday 21 December 1937, Bryant's condition
suddenly worsened, and on the Sunday he was taken to
the Yeatman Hospital in Sherborne, where he died the
same day at the age of 39. He had been an inoffensive
little man for whom nothing had gone right since he left
the Army. His passing was mourned only by his children,
and certainly not by Charlotte, who was still hoping to get
Parsons back.

If she had not administered that third and ultimately
fatal dose before she had gone to the gypsy encampment,
Charlotte might well have hesitated before she made that
last attempt to kill her husband. As it was, the next course
of events was to give her something else to think about,
other than trying to get Parsons back. To begin with, Dr
McCarthy had suddenly decided that Bryant's attacks of
violent stomach pains might have been caused by something other than the gastroenteritis he had diagnosed.
Coldly, he informed her that he could not give her a death
certificate, and that a post mortem would have to be held.

When this was carried out by Dr Roche Lynch, a distin-
guished Home Office pathologist, he found more than
four grains of arsenic in the body. As soon as the Dorset
Police had been informed of his findings they immediately
sought the aid of Scotland Yard, who sent down a team of
policemen and detectives. Before the bewildered widow

had time to fully realize what was going on, a combined team of the Dorset Police and Scotland Yard had swooped down on the Bryant home. Charlotte and her children were bundled off to the workhouse in Sturminster, where they were kept for the next seven weeks while the police searched the house and dug up the garden.

Although the police were convinced that they were dealing with a murder case, their search produced no hard evidence. Detective Sergeant Tapsell of Scotland Yard had found traces of arsenic in the samples of dust and dirt that had been carefully swept from the shelves, but this in itself was not enough to bring Charlotte to trial, as he knew that arsenic in one form or another was often kept in a farm labourer's cottage. Even a battered empty tin of weedkiller the police found in the garden was not enough to convict Charlotte unless it could be proved that she herself had purchased it. More by luck than judgement, she seemed to have got away with it, unless the police came up with something else.

Then the police had a piece of luck that changed everything. After examining the poison register books of dozens of local pharmacists, they eventually found the one they were looking for. It belonged to a Yeovil chemist who told them that he had sold a tin of arsenical weedkiller to a woman who had signed his poison register with a cross. Putting aside the fact that there seems to have been a large loophole in the law which allows such a signature without the pharmacist asking for evidence of the purchaser's name, this was enough to put the police on the right track.

It was at this point that Mrs Lucy Ostler, a widow who had become friendly with Charlotte, began to play her part in bringing about the arraignment of Charlotte Bryant. More than anyone else, she contributed to Charlotte's eventual conviction. For some reason known only to herself, Mrs Ostler had taken to Charlotte, despite her unkempt and unwashed look. She had occasionally stayed at the Bryants' house to keep Charlotte company during

Frederick's last illness. As she was not only close to her, but had even lived in the house for part of the time that Bryant was ill, she was considered a suspect as well as Charlotte. Both women were asked to appear in an identity parade, but the Yeovil pharmacist was unable to identify the woman who had bought the weedkiller.

But the identity parade had not been entirely a waste of time. Now thoroughly alarmed at having to appear in the line-up, Mrs Ostler was only too willing to give the police all the help she could when they questioned her. She told them of the occasion when Charlotte had shown her a green tin, saying, 'I must get rid of that.' A few days later she had found the same tin among the ashes in the boiler and had thrown it out into the backyard. This was the tin which had contained arsenic and which the police had found in the garden. Mrs Ostler also told them that Mrs Bryant had frequently said how much she hated her husband; and described the occasion soon after Frederick's death when Charlotte had suddenly come out with the remark, 'If they can't find anything, they can't hang me.' It was a surprising comment for a supposedly innocent woman to make, and one that seemed to indicate that Charlotte was anticipating a police enquiry. Technically speaking, all this was not substantial enough 'evidence' to hang Charlotte Bryant, but the police now felt that they had enough to send her to trial.

On 10 February 1936, Charlotte Bryant was arrested and charged with the murder of her husband. She was led away in tears and protesting her innocence, crying out, 'I never got any poison from anywhere, and that people do know. I don't see how they can say I poisoned my husband.' Mrs Ostler could for one, as she made clear at the trial. If ever there was a friend that Charlotte Bryant could have done without at that time, it was Mrs Ostler.

The trial of Charlotte Bryant began on 23 May 1936, in Dorchester, where she was brought before Mr Justice MacKinnon. Acting for the prosecution was the Solicitor

General, Sir Terence O'Connor, while the defence was to be conducted by J.D. Caswell, KC. When Charlotte was brought up from the cells, an almost perceptible murmur of disbelief greeted her arrival in the dock. Was this the woman who had once attracted men to her like bees around a honeypot? The impending case had already been well covered at the time by the press, with its usual lack of discretion, and people were already well aware of most of the circumstances which had brought the accused to trial. What they were not expecting was the sight of this unlovely, unkempt and slovenly-looking woman who now sat in the dock staring vacantly into space while the prosecution and the defence rustled through their papers in preparation for the legal battle ahead.

The Solicitor General opened the case against Charlotte, knowing that one vital piece of evidence was missing – at no time had the police been able to establish that Charlotte Bryant had ever bought arsenic in any form.

But the prosecution did have one ace in the pack – the evidence of Mrs Ostler, who was now its chief witness. In the witness box she recalled that when she was reading out the details of a famous poisoning case to Charlotte, she had suddenly interrupted her to ask, 'How would *you* get rid of someone?' She also recalled the occasion when she was staying in the house when Charlotte had given an OXO drink to her husband, who was violently sick immediately afterwards. When it came to the empty tin of weedkiller that now stood among the exhibits, she told the court that the word 'poison' had been on the lid, and stared at the empty tin significantly. One has the feeling that Mrs Ostler was rather relishing the limelight – especially as her evidence was helping to bring a murderess to justice.

Her self-righteous manner was punctured when she had to face Mr Caswell, who began quietly enough. 'You realize that the evidence you have been giving is very unfavourable to Mrs Bryant?'

'I do,' Mrs Ostler said smugly.

Mr Caswell looked at her appraisingly before going on. 'I suggest to you that your story of the tin is a falsehood.'

'It's not,' Mrs Ostler said indignantly.

'When Mr Bryant had his final and fatal illness, were not you and Mrs Bryant the only two adults in the house?'

'Yes,' Mrs Ostler admitted.

'Therefore you were in a position to administer the poison yourself?'

Mrs Ostler flushed, and had to agree with him.

This attack against Mrs Ostler was all very well as a diversionary tactic, but the one essential factor that might have caused the jury to pause before being too quick to condemn Charlotte was missing. Mrs Ostler had no motive.

Mr Caswell's moment of triumph, such as it was, was short-lived. An insurance agent named Tuck testified that he had called at the house while Charlotte was at the hospital collecting her dead husband's clothes. He was about to go away when he ran into her coming back from the hospital in the company of Mrs Ostler. 'He's gone,' Charlotte told Tuck. 'I've been a good wife to him – nobody can say I haven't. And nobody can say that I poisoned him.'

Tuck had thought at the time that it was an odd remark for her to make, and more or less said so. 'Why should they?'

'You never know what will come of these things,' Charlotte said cryptically.

Then there was the evidence of her two eldest children, aged twelve and ten, who were put in the witness stand, but as their evidence was of so little help, either to the defence or the prosecution, one wonders why they were called on to appear in the first place. Their presence moved the judge to tears, as it did a number of people in the court-room. Mrs Bryant also wept, but this made little impression on the jury.

Another witness who did Charlotte a great deal of harm was Mr Priddle, Bryant's employer, who had visited the house during the last stages of his fatal illness, and had been shocked by Charlotte's uncaring manner. What made matters even worse for the accused was the evidence of Dr Roche Lynch who had analysed the ashes in the boiler and had found an abnormal amount of arsenic in them. In his final summing up, the judge was to lay particular stress on Roche Lynch's evidence.

Charlotte sat all through this as if in a daze, only really coming to life when Parsons took the witness stand. Under questioning, he admitted freely that he had had sexual intercourse frequently with Charlotte from the day they met until he had left. He also recalled an occasion when he heard Charlotte ask her husband what was in the tin he was holding in his hand.

'That's weedkiller,' Bryant had told her.

Later, Mr Caswell managed to soften the impact of that remark on the jury by getting Parsons to admit that he had not actually seen the tin at the time.

In all, the prosecution produced thirty witnesses who all had something to say either about her squalid affair with Parsons, or about her off-hand treatment of her husband. Not one of them produced a single piece of damning evidence, but the total effect of what they had said did nothing to make the jury look with more favour on the haggard wretch in the dock.

Before going out to consider their verdict, the jury was told by the judge that they had to answer two simple questions in their minds before reaching a verdict: Did Bryant die of arsenical poisoning? And if he did, was the poison administered by his wife? The jury's mind was already made up, and they returned with their verdict within sixty minutes. They found Charlotte guilty as charged, and she was sentenced to death on Saturday 30 May 1936.

Most defence lawyers must feel they have failed their client when they have lost a case, however much the odds are stacked against them. Mr Caswell was no exception. After the trial he had gone away for the weekend in a despondent mood. But when he arrived home on the Monday, a dramatically worded letter was awaiting him that gave fresh hope for his client.

It was from a Professor William Bone of the Imperial College of Science and Technology, and it read:

Dear Sir,
If I am right in supposing that you were the Defending Counsel in the case of Rex v. Bryant, could you please communicate with me as soon as possible because I have something to put before you arising from that part of the evidence in the judge's summing up relating to the normal percentage of arsenic in the coal ashes, which I think may possibly have an important bearing upon the ultimate issue. And I would be glad of the opportunity of putting it before you in the interests of justice.

Mr Caswell immediately contacted Professor Bone, who told him that the evidence that Dr Roche Lynch had given in court was inaccurate. According to the Professor it had been established since 1900 that the proportion of arsenic normally found in the ashes of domestic fires amounted to less than 140 parts per million. In his statement Dr Roche Lynch had said that the ashes in the boiler had contained 149 parts to the million, and that this was an abnormal amount to find, and therefore suggested that arsenic had been put in the fire. In actual fact, the Professor maintained, the amount of arsenic contained in the ashes was perfectly consistent with what was normally found. In Mr Caswell's and the Professor's opinion, this destroyed one of the main props of the prosecution.

Professor Bone provided a signed statement to this effect, and Mr Caswell included it in his appeal and asked that Professor Bone's evidence should be heard by the Court of Criminal Appeal. To Mr Caswell's amazement,

Bone's evidence was rejected on the grounds that the evidence against Mrs Bryant was overwhelming.

Now irrevocably condemned to die on the scaffold, Charlotte Bryant took the news quietly and went back to her cell in Exeter Prison to await her fate at the hands of the hangman.

During her last days on earth, Charlotte passed much of the time learning to read and write. Towards the end she dictated a telegram to King Edward VIII, asking for mercy. As was customary, the telegram was not passed on, but was given to the Home Secretary, who decided that justice must take its course. Her hair now turned white, Charlotte Bryant went to keep her appointment with the hangman on the morning of 15 July, 1936. Throughout her time in the condemned cell she had steadfastly refused to see her children. She left them a legacy of five shillings and eighteen pence halfpenny which was shared out among them by the Dorset County Council which had adopted them.

There was a strange coda to Charlotte's last moments. Just before she was led out to die, she dictated the following letter:

It's all — fault I am here. I listened to the tales I was told. But I have not long now and I will be out of all my troubles. God bless the children.

To whom was she referring in this last note? To Parsons, who had encouraged her to think that he might marry her, when he had no intention of doing so? Or to Mrs Ostler, whose evidence had done so much to harm her in the court-room? We shall never know, as the prison authorities had blacked out the name of the person Charlotte had blamed for her fate.

Although Charlotte never confessed to the murder, it is fairly obvious that she was guilty. All the same, it does seem an injustice was done by the Court of Criminal Appeal in refusing to hear Professor Bone's evidence. It is

this high-handed refusal to accept certain evidence which
has led to more than one innocent person being sent to
the gallows or to prison for life.

THE SAUSAGE KING

Adolph Luetgert

American murder case 1897

Adolph Luetgert would have made an ideal model for one of those First World War propaganda posters in which the 'beastly Hun' was depicted as a brutish and sub-human monster with the sort of face that gave women and children nightmares. An enormously fat man who turned the scales at almost twenty stone, Luetgert's own bloated face was the colour of suet, from which peered a pair of pig-like eyes. To complete the wartime image of a beer-swilling, Frankfurter-loving German, he was also a sausage maker.

He had emigrated to the United States in the 1870s and had made his home in Chicago, a city which had seen him as a welcome addition to its already large German population. They might have been less keen to have him if they had known what type of man he really was. One of the many unattractive sides to his nature was his gargantuan appetite for sex.

It is one thing to want to possess every woman in sight as Luetgert did, but quite another to have any luck with a single one of them if you were as repulsive as he was. Yet strangely, his track record with women was nothing short of amazing. By the time he had decided to murder his wife he had bedded not just the occasional woman, but literally dozens of them. Finding that his sexual activities were beginning to interfere with his work, Luetgert had a bed installed in his office so that he could lumber out from between the sheets and reach the factory floor in a matter of seconds. This may have made him feel he was contributing to the efficiency of his factory, but it did nothing for the morale of his workers, who cringed whenever they saw Luetgert bearing down on them like a Prussian officer on the rampage. In this he was little different from Fred Oesterreich (see Chapter 2, 'The Cupboard Lover').

Considering the number of women who always seemed to be at his disposal, Luetgert's wife was a surprising choice. Her name was Louisa, and whatever looks she might have had were long gone. She was now an unattractive woman who slapped around the house in down-at-heel carpet slippers, and seemed to have her hair in curlers for most of the day – definitely not the sort of woman to raise the blood pressure of someone like Luetgert, who was now barely on speaking terms with her. Finding himself in the enviable position of being spoilt for choice, Luetgert had recently decided that he could do much better for himself elsewhere. First, though, Louisa would have to be sent on her way.

In January 1897, Luetgert went to see Captain Herman Schuettler who was in charge of the Sheffield Avenue Police Station. What he had to tell the captain made him look at Luetgert in some amazement. Plain, dowdy Louisa was having an affair with another man.

'We are old friends, you and I,' Luetgert said. 'I love Louisa dearly, and I want to know if there is any way I can stop her seeing this man.'

'It is not a police matter,' Schuettler told him. 'Therefore there is nothing I can do to help you. Nor can I advise you how you should handle the matter yourself.' He tried to prevent himself from smiling. 'If I may say so, your reputation for having affairs with women has become something of a scandal. So perhaps you should not complain too much.'

Luetgert rose heavily to his feet. 'I trust you will keep our conversation a private one, Captain Schuettler.'

'Of course,' Captain Schuettler said gravely.

Within days the whole neighbourhood knew that Louisa was having an affair with another man, a piece of information that caused great amusement to those who knew Luetgert. He did not share in the general amusement. He no longer spent his spare time downing tankards of lager in local bars, but chose instead to stay brooding at home. He spent less and less time in his house, and eventually took to sleeping in the factory, where he now also kept his four Great Danes.

What Louisa thought of all this is anybody's guess – especially as she had no secret lover. He had been concocted by Luetgert as part of the plan to get rid of his wife. As it was, Louisa was content enough to let things be, with her husband only visiting the house occasionally. She was well aware of the many women in her husband's life, and was long past caring what he did.

What did concern her was the financial state of A.L. Luetgert's Sausage Works. The latest trading figures were so bad that the bank had now become extremely concerned about the size of Mr Luetgert's loan. Luetgert was only too well aware that he was already practically bankrupt, but there was nothing he could do about it. Chicago had already become one of the largest meat-packing capitals of the world, killing, processing and packaging more than two-thirds of the cattle it received, and sending it out at prices Luetgert could not afford to match. All this must have been very worrying, but for the time being he was much more concerned with his plans to get rid of Louisa.

Having cut himself off from most of his drinking companions, he became friendly with his nightwatchman, a man named Frank Bialk,' who had worked for him for years. This was not an example of Luetgert becoming unexpectedly democratic with his staff, but was all part of the scheme to show all those around him how upset he was over Louisa's affair with another man.

In one of his evening conversations with Bialk he suddenly became lachrymose about his wife. 'She is being unfaithful to me, Mr Bialk,' he said mournfully. 'Even worse, I think that at any moment she is going to leave me.'

Bialk made appropriate sounds of sympathy. 'Why do you not speak to this man?' Bialk said. 'Then perhaps he will have the decency to go.'

'I would,' Luetgert said. 'But I don't know who he is. Louisa won't give me his name.'

For some time now, Luetgert had been careful not to have any women spending the night with him at his office. To have done so would have negated whatever sympathy he fancied he had managed to build up for himself as the injured husband. But for a man with his insatiable sexual appetite, the situation was fast becoming too much to bear. Late one evening he invited over one of the local matrons with whom he had slept before. Unfortunately for Luetgert she arrived when Bialk was doing his rounds. Bialk drew his own conclusions, but said nothing.

In April that year, two representatives from the bank came to see Luetgert. They made a tour of the factory and then went to see him in his office, where a stormy interview took place. After they had gone, Luetgert emerged, his normally suet-coloured complexion having taken on the distinctive beetroot-red look of a man who was just about to have a heart attack.

On 30 April, he summoned one of his employees named Oderofsky to his office. 'There's something I would like you to do,' he said. He led the way to the basement where there stood four large wooden vats in which the meat was brought to the boil with piped steam. Luetgert pointed to some sacks containing large quantities of some chunky, grey-looking substance. 'I want you to break all that stuff up and put it all in one of the vats. And be sure to wear gloves when you handle it. Otherwise you'll burn your hands badly.'

Oderofsky was curious. 'What is it, Mr Luetgert?'

Luetgert gave him an odd smile. 'Just something I'm using for an experiment. Now get on with it.' Oderofsky did as he was told, while Luetgert went away to deal with other matters.

The next morning the bank did what it had been threatening to do for some time. It closed Luetgert down. Acting on behalf of the bank, a representative from the sheriff's office visited the factory and handed him a closing-down order which told him that he and his employees were to be out of the factory in three days. By noon, Luetgert had paid off all his workers and sent them on their way. Watching the last of them go, Luetgert breathed an enormous sigh of relief that he had already started dealing with the matter of getting rid of Louisa.

When the nightwatchman checked in that evening, he was surprised to find Luetgert busily firing the furnace under one of the vats. He thought this strange at the time, since Luetgert normally boiled up the meats during the day time.

Luetgert was still busy working the furnaces when Bialk passed him later in the evening. 'Get me a stein of beer,' Luetgert called after him. 'Have one yourself while you're there. There's no need to hurry back.'

Bialk returned to the factory around 11.00 that night and found Luetgert in the process of tightening the lid on one of the vats. To his surprise, when he returned at 6.00 the following morning just prior to finishing off his shift, Luetgert was still there, busily removing the ashes from the furnace. 'I'm going home now,' the nightwatchman told him.

'I've still much to do,' Luetgert said. 'I shall probably be clearing this vat out for most of the day.' It was then that he told Bialk that the factory was closing down. 'Come to the office and I'll pay you off.'

The next day Luetgert visited Mrs Mueller, his sister-in-law. 'Is Louisa staying with you? I saw her when I got home last night, but when I went to work this morning she was gone.'

'She's not here,' Mrs Mueller assured him.

Luetgert then dragged his enormous bulk around to the Sheffield Avenue Police Station and asked to see Captain Schuettler.

'She's gone!' he announced dramatically when Schuettler arrived. 'Just as I said she would.'

'What do you expect me to do about it?' Schuettler asked.

'You allowed this to happen,' Luetgert shouted. 'Now get her back for me.' It was soon established that Louisa had left, and, moreover, was not even living in the neighbourhood. At first Captain Schuettler was not greatly concerned over Louisa's disappearance. If Louisa had indeed gone off with another man, as Luetgert claimed, he considered that Luetgert had only got what he deserved. He did not have the first twinge of unease until he had a visit from Louisa's brother, Dietrich Bickenese, a dairy farmer who lived on the outskirts of Chicago.

'I'm worried about my sister, Louisa Luetgert,' he informed the captain. 'She was supposed to have been visiting us a few days ago, but she didn't turn up. Now my brother-in-law tells me she has run off with another man. I find that rather difficult to believe.'

So did Captain Schuettler. The more he thought about it, the more he began to have the feeling that there was much more to Louisa's disappearance than Luetgert would have him believe. For some reason he could never explain afterwards, Captain Schuettler decided to make a visit to Luetgert's now-deserted factory. It was a somewhat eerie experience, walking through a building which had once been filled with the hum of the voices of the packers on Luetgert's rather primitive assembly lines. As he walked slowly through the building, Captain Schuettler could almost feel sorry for Luetgert, who had been deprived of his livelihood almost at the single stroke of a pen. He had almost completed his tour of inspection when he detected an unpleasant smell coming from the basement.

As he went down into the basement the smell became

much stronger, causing the captain to gag slightly as he looked around him, trying to find where it came from. He decided that it came from one of the vats.

He went back to Luetgert's office, where, after a great deal of searching, he came upon a woman's purse. It contained nothing more than a few dollars and cents and a small piece of neatly folded paper. This turned out to be a grocery bill with the customer's name on it. Schuettler put the receipted bill in his pocket and left the building in a thoughtful mood.

He had no difficulty in tracing the owner of the grocery bill, who turned out to be a man-hunting widow. When she became aware that an official police enquiry was in progress she talked freely, admitting that she had slept at Luetgert's office on several occasions, including the week when Luetgert's wife had disappeared. When he left her, Schuettler was in an even more thoughtful frame of mind.

From his conversation with the widow he had learned that despite Luetgert's alleged grief over his wife's departure, it had not prevented him from seeking consolation in another woman's arms. This proved nothing in itself. Luetgert had been under a great deal of stress at the time, having just lost both his business and his wife. But it did set Schuettler to wondering about a number of things which had not greatly engaged his attention before – most of them concerning Louisa, a woman who seemed a most unlikely person to suddenly run off with another man. Knowing something also of Luetgert's attitude to women, it now seemed to him in retrospect that Luetgert's grief over losing Louisa was very much out of character.

Schuettler was one of those dogged policemen who had been trained to know the value of painstaking footwork. Among the many employees from the factory whom he interviewed was Oderofsky, who recalled how Luetgert had ordered him to put vast quantities of some unknown substance in one of the vats.

'You've no idea what that substance was?' Schnettler asked.

'Only that it was something that burnt your hands badly if you didn't wear gloves.'

Convinced now that Luetgert had murdered his wife and had then disposed of the body in one of the steam vats, Schuettler went on to discuss the matter with a chemist, who came up with the interesting suggestion that Luetgert could have used potash to get rid of the body. This substance, when mixed with water and then brought to the boil, could reduce a body to a porridge-like consistency in a matter of a few hours, and reduce it to practically nothing if it was boiled in the vat for a much longer period.

When Schuettler spoke to the nightwatchman and learned that he had seen Luetgert stoking up the furnace under one of the steam vats, he decided that he now had enough circumstantial evidence to put forward a case to State's Attorney, Charles Deneen.

Deneen listened attentively to what Schuettler had to say. When he had finished, he nodded in agreement. 'The trouble is, how do you prove it?'

'I'd better start by having that steam boiler examined,' Schuettler said.

Before he was able to organize a secret examination of the vat, Schuettler had an unexpected visitor. It was none other than Luetgert, who came storming into his office in a fist-pounding mood.

Schuettler looked at him with ill-disguised hostility. 'What do you want?'

'I want a warrant sworn out for the arrest of my wife.'

'On what charge?'

Luetgert brought down a ham-like fist on the desk. 'On a charge of desertion.'

'You can't do that,' Schuettler said coldly. 'Not when you've been carrying on with someone yourself.' He mentioned the name of the woman he had recently interviewed.

'I hardly know her!' Luetgert said indignantly.

After he had gone, Schuettler set about making his plans for a night raid on Luetgert's old factory. It was essential at this stage that Luetgert should remain unaware that he was under suspicion. When it was dark a number of the windows were blacked out, and the nightwatchman and Oderofsky were sneaked into the building, followed closely by Schuettler and one of his detectives. With the nightwatchman leading the way they went to the cellar where Bialk pointed out the vat where he had seen Luetgert at work. The detective lowered himself into the vat, noting that it had been completely washed out so that it was now quite impossible to tell what substance had last been used in it. When he emerged again he had with him some minute pieces of bone and two gold rings, one of them engraved with the initials LL – Louisa Luetgert.

'I think we've got him,' Schuettler said with quiet satisfaction. 'Now let's see if the State's Attorney agrees that we've enough to nail him.'

Before Schuettler had time to see the State's Attorney, Luetgert visited him early the next morning. 'I want it to be known around that I'm giving a reward of $50 to anyone who can give me information that will lead to me finding my wife,' he announced.

'That has nothing to do with me,' Schuettler said curtly. 'Now, if you'll excuse me, I have work to do.' He watched Luetgert go before phoning to make an appointment to see Charles Deneen. When Deneen was told what had been found in Luetgert's old factory, he agreed there was enough circumstantial evidence for them to arrest Luetgert. 'Don't expect it's going to be a cut and dried case,' he warned the police captain. 'When it comes to it, we have only the initialled ring that is worth anything in court. Still – it's worth trying.'

Luetgert was arrested later that day and led away, loudly protesting his innocence. Fortunately, when it came to the trial, the State's Attorney was able to produce a number of Luetgert's mistresses, who all testified against him, including one who claimed that Luetgert had given her a bloodstained knife to look after. Despite a spirited defence by W.A. Vincent, Luetgert was found guilty and sentenced to life imprisonment. More than anything else it was the gold ring with the initials of Luetgert's wife which finished him. There must have been many in the courtroom that day who blanched at the thought that Louisa might have been still alive when Luetgert put her in the vat and slowly boiled her away, until all that was left of her were a few fragments of bone and her gold rings.

Luetgert served his sentence in Joliet State Penitentiary, where he died in 1911, still claiming he was innocent.

MR ROUSE ARRANGES HIS OWN DEATH

Alfred Rouse

English murder 1930

Alfred Rouse was a man with an enormous sexual appetite that compelled him to pursue every woman who was unwise enough to show even the slightest interest in him. Some of them he married bigamously, others he kept dangling with promises of marriage which he was in no position to honour. A compulsive liar with a persuasive and charming manner, he continued going up and down the country, seducing women until he eventually found himself in a situation where he had to disappear to escape from his pursuers and possible imprisonment for bigamy. The course of action he took was one that turned him from an inveterate womanizer into a callous killer.

Born on 6 April 1894, Rouse was brought up in an unhappy house of warring parents. When they separated, he was committed by his father to the care of his sister, who brought him up from the age of six. After attending the local council school at Herne Hill, where he had shown a talent for music, he went to evening classes and learned to play the piano, violin and mandolin. At this point he seems to have been a sensitive youth who might well have found a niche for himself as a professional musician. Instead, he virtually abandoned that idea and went to work in a West End store, where he attended to the customers in the soft furnishings department.

He was obviously a patriotic young man, for when war broke out in 1914, he immediately enlisted in the 24th Queen's Regiment as a private. By then he was already courting Lily May Watkins, who was to remain faithful to him to the end. He married her before going overseas, where he was to see a great deal of action in northern France before he returned home, having been badly wounded in the head by shrapnel.

So far he could be said to have been a model if undistinguished citizen. What changed him to the man he was to become? It has been said that the injuries he sustained to the head in the war may have been responsible for certain personality changes, including his sudden voracious sexual appetite. There may have been some truth in this, as none of the unlikable aspects of his character had been apparent before the war.

This extraordinary personality change began to manifest itself as soon as he became a commercial traveller for a Leicester firm. Instead of music, he now became fascinated with cars. Travelling up and down the country, he soon became a first-class driver and an expert mechanic.

Although he had bought a modest home for his wife and himself in Buxted Road, Finchley, his wife saw little of him. The very nature of his job took him out of London a great deal, and provided an ideal opportunity for him to follow his new obsession – that of pursuing women. In this he was no different to many commercial travellers who use their job as a means to having extra-marital affairs. The difference with Rouse was that he used it to create a veritable harem of unhappy women who waited patiently for him to see them the next time he was in the district. With more than eighty women on his visiting list, Rouse must have travelled around in a state of near physical exhaustion for most of the time.

The long chain of self-made misfortunes began when he met and made pregnant a fifteen-year-old girl, whom he had first met in Edinburgh when she was only fourteen and had continued to see from time to time whenever he was in the city. When she became pregnant by him, she was put in a home for unmarried mothers, where the child was born and died when it was only a few weeks old. As with so many of his conquests from all over the country,

Rouse kept in touch with the girl, and in 1924 went through a form of marriage with her. It was the first of his bigamous marriages. More were to follow before his eventual arrest.

When his first bigamous marriage produced a second child, Rouse inexplicably confessed to the mother that he was married already, and arranged for her to meet his long-suffering legal wife, who agreed to raise the child in the Rouse household.

After an experience like that, any normal man would have been very careful about his future behaviour. But Rouse was not a normal man. Completely devoid of any moral principles, he carried on just as he had done before, picking up and seducing young and attractive girls, mostly from the lower middle classes. The fact that they were often under age, or barely out of their teens, made no difference to Rouse. All of them were there only to be seduced, a task which he always undertook with the boundless enthusiasm of a modern-day Casanova.

Inevitably, there were some serious casualties. First there was a seventeen-year-old servant girl who was living in Hendon when he met her in 1925. After telling her that he was single and therefore available, he persuaded her to travel with him around the country for a while in his Morris Minor, while promising to marry her as soon as his financial position improved. When she bore him a baby girl in 1928, she immediately slapped a maintenance order on Rouse, who was easily traceable through his work. This did not stop her from continuing to sleep with him from time to time, and in 1928 she conceived another child by him.

Rouse, meanwhile, had been his usual busy self elsewhere, and had gone through another marriage ceremony with Ivy Jenkins in Monmouthshire. This time he made the mistake of visiting her parents, who were informed that Rouse had already bought and furnished a fine house for their daughter in Kingston. Unlike their daughter, who

had been completely bowled over by Rouse, they were
suspicious of this smooth-tongued stranger. Neither the
father or the girl's brother voiced their unease about the
wedding, which had been something of a shotgun affair,
but their hostility was all too evident. They were slightly
placated when Rouse suggested that his new wife's sister
might care to live with them until the new bride had
become used to married life.

After he had left them, Rouse knew he was in deep
trouble. He could tell that the family had been unim-
pressed with his fanciful tales of having an education at
Eton and Cambridge before being commissioned as a
major in the First World War. He had also gained the
impression that the father and son were a vengeful pair
who would make him pay dearly if he failed to honour all
his promises to his new wife.

It was a nightmare dilemma, and he could see only one
way out of it, and that was to disappear. By doing so he
could rid himself of the rising tide of debts that were now
threatening to engulf him, while at the same time ridding
himself of all the encumbrances with which he had
saddled himself over the years. But this was more easily
said than done, especially if you were a man with Rouse's
track record. Wronged women all over the country might
identify him at any time if he took the simple way out by
merely changing his name. His twisted mind conceived an
elaborate plan which included leaving the country, but
only after he had been declared officially dead in England.
Considering that he was obviously unhinged, his plan was
a highly ingenious one that might just have worked if it
had not been for those elements in his nature which were
to destroy him when he most needed a cool head and a
quiet tongue.

His plan entailed finding a man of about the same
height and build as himself, and one, moreover, who
would never be missed if he were to suddenly disappear.
By an incredible chance he found the very man he was

looking for when he was accosted in the street by a shabbily dressed stranger asking him for money. Although he never drank himself, Rouse took the stranger to a nearby pub and plied him with drink, while he listened to the man's tale of woe.

'I'm out of work,' the man confided in him. 'I've tried finding work in Peterborough, Norwich, and even Hull, all without any luck. I just don't know what to do next. I haven't even any relatives I can go to until something turns up.'

Rouse's eyes gleamed. He had just found the perfect victim. 'I'm going to Leicester tomorrow,' he said. 'Why don't you try there? If you're interested, I'd be glad to take you with me.'

The stranger readily agreed, and Rouse arranged to meet him the next evening in the same public house. Some time after eight that evening the two men met as they had arranged, and they drove off into the night, after Rouse had bought a bottle of whisky so that his companion could drink himself into insensibility before Rouse coolly murdered him.

It is interesting to conjecture what Rouse would have done if he had not met the stranger, who was never identified. Would his resolve have weakened if he had not found such a readily available victim? The chances are that once his initial panic over his desperate situation had subsided, he might well have gone on as he had always done, before he was ultimately found out and put in prison for bigamy – something infinitely preferable to ending up dangling on the end of the hangman's noose.

But as soon as he drove away from that public house on the night of 6 November 1930, Rouse was committed to a course of action which was to make the Blazing Car Mystery, as it became known, one of the most celebrated cases in the history of British crime. He drove in the direction of St Albans, while his companion drank steadily from the whisky bottle until he was no longer able to carry on a coherent conversation. When he eventually fell into a drunken sleep, Rouse turned into a lane near the main road where he was hoping he could thumb a lift once his dreadful work was completed. He then stopped the car and proceeded to throttle his intoxicated companion, who gurgled helplessly for a few minutes before his death.

Once he was sure his victim was dead, Rouse got out of the car, taking with him his attaché case and the can of petrol which he had put in the back of the car. He doused his victim with the petrol, loosened the petrol union joint and the top of the carburettor, and then made a petrol trail before replacing the can. Afterwards, he put a match to the petrol trail and watched it race to the car. Within seconds the car was blazing furiously. He watched until his victim was engulfed in flames before hurrying away, convinced he had committed the perfect crime.

It was then that his plans suddenly began to go wrong. Two young cousins, Alfred and William Bailey, had gone to a dance that evening in Northampton, and were on the last stage of their journey home on foot back to their village when they became aware that something was on fire further down the lane. Almost at the same time they saw Rouse hurrying towards them.

'What's happened?' one of the cousins asked him.

'It looks as if someone is having a bonfire,' Rouse called out as he hurried past them.

That chance encounter in the early hours of the morning had shaken Rouse badly, and he was no longer sure of himself. On the main road to London he managed to hitch a lift from a lorry and by 6.30 in the morning he was home in London. By then he had become panic-stricken and unable to think clearly, though on his journey back in the lorry he must have had time to realize that he had made a terrible mistake in not showing more interest in the blazing car. The cousins could not possibly have seen him clearly enough in the dark to identify his face from a photograph, but the very fact that a man had been seen hurrying away from the blazing car would be enough to make the police wonder if Rouse had indeed been burnt to death in his car.

While in this disturbed state of mind, Rouse made another and even more fatal error. He had received a letter from his Welsh 'wife', Ivy, asking him to come and see her in the Cardiff hospital where she was about to have his child. At the time Rouse had decided to ignore the letter. Now, for some strange reason, he decided to go and see her. He spent the night with his legal wife and by the following afternoon he was on a coach travelling down to Cardiff. Considering the whole purpose of murdering the stranger had been to fake his own death in the Morris Minor, he seems to have gone about his disappearance in a very strange way.

After visiting the hospital, he went on to the Jenkins's family home in Gellygaer, picking up an evening newspaper on the way. To his horror, the story of the discovery of the burnt-out car had made the headlines, rather than being a small item tucked away in the middle of the paper as he had hoped.

It was late when he reached the Jenkins's home, and he went straight to bed, where he spent a sleepless night going over the events of the last twenty-four hours. He must have realized by then that his panic-stricken behaviour had led to a series of disastrous mistakes that could cost him his life. Worse was soon to follow.

When he got up the next morning and went downstairs, it was to find Phyllis Jenkins, the sister of his 'wife', waiting for him. 'Is that your car?' Phyllis asked, pointing to a picture of his burnt-out Morris Minor, in the morning paper.

Rouse looked at the picture and then turned away. 'Oh no,' he said. 'That's not my car.'

'It must be,' Phyllis insisted. 'Your name is registered against the number plate – MU1468. The police want to see you.'

'It was stolen,' Rouse said weakly. 'I'm going to see the police as soon as I get back to London.'

He left the house soon afterwards and was given a lift to the Cardiff coach station by a Mr Brownhill with whom he had had a conversation about his burnt-out car.

'How did the accident happen?' Mr Brownhill asked him.

'It's too long to go into,' Rouse said evasively. 'I'm telling the police all about it when I reach London.'

We do not know whether it was Phyllis, Mr Brownhill, or someone else from the village who told the police that Rouse was on his way to London by coach. But someone did, for when the coach reached Hammersmith it was intercepted by Detective Sergeant Skelly and two constables.

'Are you Mr Rouse?' Skelly asked, after Rouse had been told to step out of the coach. 'If so, I must ask you to accompany us to the police station.'

Rouse knew that he had reached the end of the road. 'Very well,' he said. 'I am glad it is over. I am responsible. I'm very glad it is all over.' He added plaintively, 'I have had no sleep.'

Rouse must have realized the net was already closing around him when he had stepped on the coach in Cardiff. He therefore had time to concoct a story for the police that portrayed him as a totally innocent man who had been the victim of a set of unhappy circumstances.

According to Rouse he had been hailed by a man on the Great North Road who was making for the Midlands. As Rouse was heading in that direction he was happy to give him a lift. They were near St Albans when Rouse had felt the need to relieve himself and had turned off into a quiet lane, where he had stopped the car. 'There's some petrol in a can at the back,' he said. 'You can empty it into the tank while I'm gone.'

'What about a smoke?' his companion had called out while he was lifting the bonnet. Although he was a nonsmoker, Rouse very conveniently happened to have a cigar in his pocket which had been given him by one of his clients. He handed it to the stranger and then went on down the lane until he found a quiet spot where he could relieve himself. He had just finished when he saw a light, followed by a large sheet of flame coming from the direction of where he had left his car. By the time he reached the vehicle it was enveloped in flames. Seeing his passenger sitting inside he tried to open the door, only to be beaten back by the heat of the flames. Panic-stricken, and no longer capable of any logical thought, he fled without even seeking help from the two cousins, as he ran to the highway where he had thumbed a lift to London.

This statement, which he repeated to the Northampton police when they arrived the next morning, was so full of holes that even Rouse had the sense later to realize that they made the outcome of his trial a certainty. His attempts to justify his story only confirmed in everybody's minds that he was a pathological liar whose every statement needed to be put under a microscope. Inspector Lawrence of the Northampton police wisely left it to the experts to demolish Rouse's story in court.

By the time he was brought to trial at the Northampton Assizes on 26 January 1931, he had recovered a good deal of his composure. His manner was almost jaunty as he took his place in dock and prepared to face the great Norman Birkett, who was appearing this time as the leading counsel for the Crown. Before he had uttered a single word in his defence, Rouse had already done himself a great deal of harm by talking freely to the police about his 'harem' and displaying an unfeeling attitude to his wife who had loyally taken a local job in Northampton so that she could be near him in his hour of need. Much of this had been reported to the press, and a great deal of hostility towards Rouse had been stirred up before he had even come to trial.

Not that Rouse seemed to need any propping up. When

he faced Birkett in court he was unpleasantly arrogant, too self-assured and too talkative for his own good, treating Birkett's loaded questions as if they were easily parried sword thrusts. Where one word would have done he used dozens, and where a dozen were needed he supplied the scribbling journalists with long paragraphs to be transcribed from their shorthand notes afterwards, all the while steadily digging his own grave.

For example, when Birkett asked him why he had not asked for help from the two cousins he had met on the road while running away from the burning car, Rouse replied, 'I lost my head and didn't know what I was doing, and I don't really know what I have done since.'

This was the weakest part of his story and Rouse knew it. He could only hope that Birkett had no more nasty moments in court in store for him. He should have known better.

'Why did you allow more than forty-three hours to pass between the time of the "accident" and the time you were taken off the coach without reporting the matter to the police?' Birkett asked him at one point.

'Because I have very little confidence in local police stations,' Rouse said. 'I was waiting until I could go to the fountainhead.' He gave Birkett a conspiratorial smile. 'One usually goes to the fountainhead when one wants things done.'

Birkett did not return the smile. 'Why did you tell Detective Sergeant Skelly that you felt "responsible" when he took you off the coach?'

'Because in the eyes of the police the owner of a car is always responsible for anything that happens to that car.' A touch of his former arrogance returned briefly as he stared at Birkett. 'Correct me if I am wrong.'

A lay person would have felt like hitting him at this point, but this was a court of law and Birkett was too much of a gentleman and a professional to show his feelings to a man who, after all, was on trial for his life.

Rouse's confident manner only really faltered once, and that was when he was handed the remains of the car's carburettor and he turned pale. It was the prosecution's contention that it had been tampered with, and despite a show of technical knowledge, Rouse was unable to prove otherwise. To make matters worse, his guilty reaction on handling the carburettor was enough for the jury to add yet another black mark against him.

In a case of this nature, where there were only the charred remains of an unknown man for the police to work on, there was very little in the way of forensic evidence, the one notable exception being something that provided Norman Birkett with a dramatic moment during the closing stages of the trial.

When the remains had been examined by Sir Bernard Spilsbury and Dr Eric Snow, a Northampton pathologist, they found that when the body had contracted as a result of being subjected to the extreme heat of the fire, it had trapped a tiny piece of cloth from the top of the left trouser leg against the trunk of the body, leaving it untouched by fire. When this one piece of surviving cloth was examined, it showed that it had been saturated in petrol, thereby proving that the body had been doused with petrol before it was set alight.

It was the final clincher to a case which had indulged the public's morbid fascination with the more ghoulish aspects of a murder case, as well as supplying them with the more titillating circumstances of Rouse's sex life.

Horrifying though the circumstances were, what antagonized the jury more than anything else was Rouse's callous attitude towards his victim, to whom he had contemptuously referred as 'the sort of man no one would miss.' Found guilty, he was sentenced to death on 31 January and, after an unsuccessful appeal, was hanged in Bedford jail on 10 March 1931. Before his execution he made a full confession which was published later in the *Daily Sketch*.

Three days before his execution, Mrs Rouse wrote the following letter:

I have fought to the last ditch to save my husband's life. But alas, I have failed, and the law will take its course. Those who knew him well knew the good that was in Arthur. I did, and so do others.

But I knew that I was fighting a lost cause, for before he went to the Court of Criminal Appeal he told me that the jury's verdict was the correct one and that he was guilty.

My own opinion is that he was not in his right mind on November 5th.

Lily May Rouse

It is hard not to feel very sorry for Mrs Rouse. After being lumbered with one of Rouse's illegitimate children, and having patiently endured his many liaisons for so long, she ended up having to sell the contents of her home and became the penniless widow of a man who was one of the most infamous criminals of the twentieth century. She deserved something better.

A BRICKBAT FOR MRS PARKER

Pauline Parker and Juliet Hulme

New Zealand murder case 1954

During the trial of Pauline Parker and Juliet Hulme, the Crown Prosecutor referred to them as 'dirty-minded girls'. In using this phrase he must have echoed the feelings of many of the citizens of Christchurch, New Zealand, a cathedral city which had all the appearances of an English market town which had somehow been transferred to the Antipodes, complete with all its deep-rooted prejudices and patterns of social behaviour. Even the outdated clothes people wore in Christchurch seemed to belong more to the English counties.

Given such a background it was hardly surprising that so many people were shocked and appalled as they learned how and why Pauline Parker and Juliet Hulme had come to murder Pauline's mother. How could two well brought-up girls behave in such a manner and become involved in such beastly unnatural acts? they asked themselves. They were soon to find out from the Crown Prosecutor, who spared them nothing as he unfolded a horrifying story in which the two girls' passion for each other had finally led them to committing murder – in Pauline's case, matricide.

The story of Pauline Parker and Juliet Hulme's fatal attraction began when they met at Christchurch Girls' Grammar School. Like so many other young girls of their age, they developed a crush on each other, only in this case it matured into a relationship with deep lesbian overtones. Of the two, Pauline was the least attractive. At sixteen she had become a dumpy, sallow girl with a slight limp after a series of operations for osteomyelitis. Juliet, on the other hand, had blossomed into an attractive fifteen-year-old girl with the assured manner of someone who had been brought up with money in the family. In those days, one's social background counted in Christchurch, where social snobbery was even more rife than it was in England.

Of the two, Juliet's background seems to have been the more secure. Her father, Dr Henry Ransford Hulme, had been one of England's major 'boffins', and had helped to work out a way to defuse the German magnetic mines that had wreaked so much damage on British shipping during the Second World War. He was considered to be a valuable asset by the War Office, and they were somewhat dismayed when he announced he was leaving England to take up the post of Rector of Canterbury University College at Christchurch. His decision had been made mainly because his daughter was suffering from tuberculosis and would benefit from living in the clean air of a country free of the industrial smog that made England so unpleasant for anyone suffering from lung or respiratory ailments.

Dr Hulme settled easily enough into his new job, but the move to New Zealand turned out to be disastrous. Among the people that Dr Hulme entertained in his home was Walter Perry, an English businessman of considerable charm. Perry became very friendly with the Hulme family, especially the wife, who found herself being irresistibly drawn to him, with dire results for her marriage. It was the old, all too familiar story of a woman who had lived happily enough with a donnish and rather stuffy husband for years, until someone had suddenly come along and seen her as something other than a middle-aged housewife and mother.

Things came to a head when Juliet came home one afternoon and found her mother in bed with Walter Perry. She said nothing to her father, but as it happened, Dr Hulme had suddenly become aware of what was happening under his very nose. He said nothing for some time, and then coldly announced that he was giving up his job and returning to England as soon as his contract had expired. His intention at the time was to take his son Jonathan with him, but leave Juliet with her mother.

Pauline's own family life had not been without its problems. In the first place her parents were not married, something that might seem of no importance today, but carried a stigma in Christchurch, where a moral code that dated back to the 1920s appertained. In addition, the couple had had four children, one of them with Down's Syndrome who had become so impossible to handle that the infant had been placed in an institution and another had been born with a congenital heart defect and had died.

Despite their initial grief, Pauline's father and his common-law wife had managed to build a reasonable, not unhappy life for themselves in Christchurch, where her father ran a wholesale fish shop. Both of them took some consolation from the fact that they still had Pauline and their other daughter, Wendy.

Neither of the two families, and least of all Mrs Parker, deserved what was soon to be inflicted on them.

It was Pauline's mother who first became aware of her daughter's association with Juliet. They had already had trouble with Pauline, who had been caught in bed with a boy named Nicholas who was staying with them at the time. Nicholas had been sent packing and Pauline given a severe talking to and reminded of the dangers of going to bed with someone without being married. But at least it had been normal enough behaviour for a girl of Pauline's age, even though she had shown a reckless disregard for the possible consequences, which made Mrs Parker shudder whenever she thought of it.

Pauline's obsession with her friend which had really begun the year before when she had started staying the night at Juliet's house, was something else again. At first

she had smiled indulgently whenever she saw them
together, thinking how nice it was that Pauline had
become friends with the daughter of an important man in
the community, who lived in a large sixteen-roomed house
standing in its own grounds. Even when Pauline had
begun to spend long hours in her friend's house, she was
not unduly worried, though she was a little upset that
Pauline seldom brought her friend to her own home,
thinking that her daughter was probably a little ashamed
of their modest home and her father's occupation.

It was not until the friendship of the two girls became
such that they were seldom out of each other's sight that
she became suspicious. Although an unworldly woman,
she was well aware that lesbian relationships existed, and
she began to wonder if Pauline was developing similar
tendencies. Deciding that the best thing she could do was
to confront the situation head on, she took Pauline to see
the family doctor, who examined Pauline and then had a
private talk with her. His verdict was an inconclusive one,
but being a practical man he made the sensible suggestion
that Pauline should be sent to a different school.

In the meantime, Dr Hulme had begun to have the
same doubts about his daughter, and had also decided that
Juliet's relationship with Pauline was an unhealthy one
which had to be broken up as soon as possible. That afternoon, he informed Juliet that he was going to South
Africa, and that he was taking her with him.

'Oh, no, Daddy!' Juliet exclaimed in dismay.

'Please, let's have no arguments,' Dr Hulme said.
'You're going.'

'No, I'm not!' Juliet said. A thought had occurred to
her. 'Not unless I can take Pauline with me.'

'Out of the question,' Dr Hulme said firmly. 'You two
see too much of each other as it is. Anyway, I'm sure that
Mrs Parker wouldn't allow her to go.'

'Yes, she would. I'm sure she would. Please, please
speak to her, Daddy,' Juliet cried hysterically.

'I shall do nothing of the sort,' Dr Hulme said. 'Now, please let's not discuss it any more. You're going!'

'I won't! I won't!' Juliet screamed hysterically, running from the room.

Pauline was upset when she heard the news, and her reaction was no less violent until she had calmed down a little. 'Don't worry, Mummy will let me go,' she assured her friend. 'She always gives in if I make enough fuss.'

It was true that Mrs Parker had always taken the easy way by giving in to most of her daughter's demands, even to the extent of letting her keep a pony which she had known was nothing more than a passing whim, occasioned by the knowledge that her friend owned a pony too. But this time she stood firm. 'I wouldn't dream of asking Dr Hulme if he would mind taking you along with him. Apart from anything else, we can't afford it.'

'I'm sure Dr Hulme wouldn't mind paying for me,' Pauline said. 'He's got oodles of money.'

'I couldn't allow him to pay for you,' Mrs Parker said indignantly. 'You'll just have to get used to doing without your precious friend.'

'Rotten cow!' Pauline flounced off, leaving her mother upset but relieved that the problem of her daughter's relationship with her friend was soon to be resolved.

But it was very far from being resolved. Neither of the families was aware of just how malignant the girls would become when they knew for certain that they would be denied each other's company, probably for ever. If there is such a thing as pure evil, then this pair could be cited as evidence that it does indeed exist.

Both of them were above average intelligence, and in many ways they lived the life of any normal middle-class girl who has been rather spoilt at home. They had both owned ponies at one time, and they both loved the cinema and were great fans of some of the popular male stars of the day, who often featured in their dreams and sexual fantasies. Pauline kept a diary and wrote poems and shared an ambition with Juliet to become a famous writer. They were also religious up to a point, and believed in life after death. So what happened?

To begin with they seemed incapable of making any sound moral judgement on a given situation. They also suffered from *folie des grandeurs*, seeing themselves as intellectually superior to anyone else. Both of them also lived most of their lives in a state of excitation, always over-reacting whenever their wishes were thwarted. None of these unfortunate characteristics, which amounted to a form of paranoia, might have mattered too much if the girls had not become friends. The combination of Pauline's contentious attitude to the world at large, and Juliet's febrile temperament exacerbated by the nature of her tubercular condition (one remaining lung was infected), made them a deadly duo when their relationship was threatened.

The word 'revenge' began to appear frequently in their conversation as they discussed *ad nauseam* Dr Hulme's idea of taking his daughter to South Africa, which he must have planned to take place during the summer recess when his contract had expired at the university.

Probably because Dr Hulme was a man and more able to defend himself against a cowardly attack, it was Mrs Parker who was chosen to be the victim of sacrifice on the altar of revenge against their parents for daring to try and keep them apart. To try and make sense of what they hoped to gain from it all would be a useless exercise, as they were now plainly mad, though the prosecution at their trial would have it otherwise.

In her diary, produced at the trial, it was obvious that Pauline did not choose her own mother as the victim until 18 April 1954, but on 28 April she made the following entry: 'Anger against Mother boiling inside me as she is the main obstacle in my path. Suddenly, means of ridding myself of the obstacle occurs to me. If she were to die –'

Soon afterwards she suggested murdering her mother to

Juliet, who obviously reacted enthusiastically to the idea, as on 20 June there was the following entry in the diary: 'Deborah and I talked for some time. Afterwards, we discussed our plans for moidering Mother and made them clear ...'

The name Deborah was one she had invented for her friend, and the use of the word 'moidering' was something that Pauline had picked up after seeing gangster movies in which a number of the characters talked in Brooklyn accents.

The last entry was on 22 July, and carried a single, chilling sentence. 'The Day of the Happy Event.'

For more than four months the two girls had nursed their resentment against their parents until it had become a festering sore that refused to heal. It was during this period they had decided to run away together to America, where they would become famous writers. To this end they had been out on a series of shoplifting expeditions, as well as systematically robbing their parents of whatever small change they could lay their hands on. What they had stolen would have paid for no more than a few local bus fares, but by now they were well past being capable of any logical thought.

On the afternoon of 22 July 1954 they were ready to murder Mrs Parker. That afternoon she had taken them out shopping, and they were now on their way home, pausing only for a cup of tea in Victoria Park before completing the last stage of the journey. Smirking, they followed Mrs Parker out of the park, exchanging conspiratorial glances as they walked demurely on either side of her.

They were strolling down a quiet country track surrounded by pine trees, when Mrs Parker exclaimed, 'How pretty!' She bent down to pick up a pink pebble, whereupon Pauline quickly brought from her pocket half a brick which had been knotted in the end of one of her stockings. Swinging the stocking like a sling shot, she

brought it down on Mrs Parker's bent head. As she
slumped to the ground with a low moan, Pauline continued to rain blows down on her head like some
demented carpet beater. Juliet, who had been walking in
front of them, came running back, and snatching the
loaded stocking from Pauline's hand, she carried on where
Pauline had left off, bringing the improvised weapon
down time and time again until Mrs Parker's head lay
absolutely smashed. Finally, she stopped, and the two of
them stared at each other over the corpse.

'We've done it,' Juliet whispered. 'Now we're free.'

The two girls fled, leaving Pauline's mother sprawled
out on the path, with blood pouring from the forty-five
wounds the girls had inflicted to her head.

When the police were called to the scene of the crime, it
had not taken much working out on their part to realize
who had committed the murder. Standing in the police
station in their blood-spattered school uniforms, Pauline
and Juliet had repeated the poor excuse of a story they
had told to all and sundry in Victoria Park, where they
had fled after reducing Mrs Parker's head to a bloody
pulp.

'She tripped and fell,' Pauline said. Seeing the police
sergeant's eyes fixed on her stained uniform, she added.
'We tried to lift and carry her. But she was too heavy –'

Their statement was so patently absurd that they were
immediately put under arrest. Three weeks later a
magistrate committed them for trial.

For weeks prior to the trial, the murder of Mrs Parker
was the main topic of conversation among the people of
Christchurch, which had always been proud of its record
of law and order in a city where most of the violence that
occurred there was meted out in a spirit of friendly rivalry
between the players in the Rugby Union Football
matches. When journalists began to fly in to cover the
case, people began to speculate on the outcome of the
trial and how it was going to affect the parents. Take the

case of the greatly respected Dr Hulme, for instance. Would he be gently eased out of his job once all the horrid and squalid details were made public knowledge in court?

Dr Hulme didn't stay to find out. By the time his daughter came to trial he had left the country, taking his son Jonathan with him. One can hardly blame him. His wife was still carrying on with Perry, and although the Hulmes had maintained the polite fiction that all was well in their marriage there was no point in staying and exposing his son to the stares and the shame of being the brother of a young murderess who had taken part in a revolting killing. On the way back to England he must have thought he was well out of it. He had no qualms whatever about leaving his wife, who was already preparing to change her name to Perry by deed poll before he had even reached England.

Mary Parker's husband was not so lucky. Day after day he had to endure sitting in court listening to the prosecution portraying his daughter as an evil young monster who had committed matricide, and for no other reason than Mrs Parker having tried to separate her from her friend. It could not have been easy either for Mrs Hulme, who was also in court. But at least she had Perry at her side to give her moral support.

It was clear from the very beginning that the Crown Prosecutor, Alan A. Brown, saw the girls as sane, cold-hearted killers who had committed the crime with malice aforethought. In his mind, there was no question that Pauline Parker and Juliet Hulme might be insane. He described the killing of Mrs Parker in such vivid detail that some of those in the court-room gasped audibly with horror.

Pauline and Juliet sat through the Prosecutor's chilling recital of the facts with the calm air of two girls listening to their headmaster reading through a list of prizewinners at the school sports. Only once did one of them react violently, and that was when the prosecution made

mention of an entry in Pauline's diary of the boy Nicholas
making a number of visits to her bedroom before they had
been caught out by Mrs Parker. Juliet's reaction to this
piece of information was one you might expect from a
lover who had just learned that her girlfriend had been
unfaithful. Glaring at Pauline, Juliet's face changed from
one of calm detachment to an expression of venomous
hatred as she leaned over and hissed something to her
friend.

To support its contention that the two girls were sane
when they committed the crime, the Crown called Dr
Stalworthy of the Avondale Mental Hospital in Auckland
to the stand. He had examined them both several times
prior to the trial, and had come to the conclusion that
neither of them suffered from paranoia and knew exactly
what they were doing when they had murdered Mrs
Parker. Another medical officer was then produced, who
supported every word of Dr Stalworthy's statement.

Despite the valiant attempts of the girls' two defence
lawyers to prove that their clients were incapable of
making any moral judgements, the jury supported the
Crown Prosecutor's final submission that 'these girls are
not incurably insane, they are incurably bad.' After being
out for more than two hours the jury came back with a
verdict of guilty, and as they were both under eighteen,
Pauline and Juliet were sentenced to be detained during
Her Majesty's pleasure. Despite the intensity of their feelings for each other, it was never really proved there had
been anything physical in their relationship.

Pauline Parker was sent to Orohata Borstal, near
Wellington, where she became a model prisoner, taking
and passing her School Certificate in her first year there.
Surprisingly, considering that she had tuberculosis, and
that Pauline had been the one who had thought up the
idea of murdering her mother in the first place, Juliet was
sent to the grim Mount Edwin Prison in Auckland, where
all prisoners sentenced to death were executed. Like

Pauline, she tried to make the best of her situation by becoming a quiet, well-behaved prisoner and spent much of her spare time writing stories and studying languages. Both of them have since been released.

To call into question the verdict at their trial is something beyond the scope of this book and would only open vast areas for discussion on a criminal system in which insanity is perhaps too rigidly defined. If the verdict now seems an unrealistic one today, one can only remind oneself that in a less enlightened age, Pauline Parker and Juliet Hulme would undoubtedly have been executed.

A PASSION FOR POISON

Nannie Doss

American murder case 1954

Most people who knew Mrs Nannie Doss would tell you that it was a treat just to be in her company. She always had a ready and cheerful smile and never had a bad word to say about anyone. She was kind to children and animals, and always took the trouble to be on good terms with her neighbours. This is not to say, of course, that she did not have her detractors, who found her gushing manner a little hard to take, especially when it was coupled with her tendency to giggle too much, a childlike habit which some felt ill became a large, over-weight woman of forty-nine. The outsider would probably merely see her as one of those typical American matrons who can be seen stomping down Main Street in any small town in the American Midwest.

Beneath that surface show of garrulous good nature, there was another side of Nannie Doss that no one knew anything about. She was an incurable romantic, whose banked fires of passion had been stoked by a constant diet of reading *True Romance*, a mass circulation magazine that aimed to bring a little pleasure into the humdrum existence of the none-too-bright housewife who had become bored out of her mind by the sight of her husband across the breakfast table. Most of these stories led to a great deal of harmless fantasizing by the magazine's readers. But with Nannie Doss it had gone much further than that. Using *True Romance* stories as her yardstick, she had turned her life into an endless quest for the perfect man, who could give her the sort of meaningful relationship that so many women yearn for. If she had

been a realistic person, Nannie would have eventually
settled for something considerably less, bearing in mind
that years of eating junk food had turned her into a somewhat gross and distinctly unfeminine figure. But such
paltry considerations had never stopped her seemingly
unending quest for Mr Right.

Nannie Doss had been married five times, and still
hadn't found her ideal. What was remarkable was not so
much her determination to find the right man, but rather
the way in which she went about it. Each time she
married, only to find her husband less than perfect, she
got rid of him by serving up a tasty dish of stewed prunes
laced with arsenic, thereby paving the way for her to try
again with someone else. In this manner she killed four of
her husbands. Having acquired the habit of poisoning
people, there was no stopping her.

The saga of Nannie Doss from Tulsa, Oklahoma, who
cut a swathe of death throughout the county, began when
she married her first husband, George Frazer. By all
accounts, he seems to have been a long-suffering man who
had suddenly found himself saddled with a fifteen-year-
old bride who kept running off with someone else once
she had decided that Frazer was not her dream man. Each
of her forays outside the marriage had ended in disaster,
and each time she had returned to her husband begging
for forgiveness, which had been freely given.

Frazer had put up with it all until he could stand no
more, and inevitably the marriage had ended in divorce,
but not before Nannie had given him three children, two
of whom had died suddenly from mysterious stomach
pains, having been poisoned by Nannie before she had
gone off with another lover named Frank Harrelson
whom she married in 1947. This was another mismatch
and lasted exactly a year before he died from some mysterious stomach complaint, after having been served a dish
of stewed prunes. Harrelson's two-year-old grandson from
a previous marriage had died in the same year, also after

being poisoned by Nannie for no discernible reason.

In the same year she met and married Arlie Lanning, another inoffensive man who was allowed to survive until 1952 before Nannie decided that the time had come to continue her search for the perfect husband, a quest that was beginning to assume the proportions of Lancelot's search for the Holy Grail. Stewed prunes was once more the method she would use to get rid of Lanning, but to make sure she had got the right culinary mix of prunes and arsenic, she first tried out the dish on Lanning's nephew who was visiting the house. The nephew passed away suddenly from food poisoning, as did Lanning shortly afterwards. Once he had been interred, with Nannie shedding copious tears at the graveside, she was free once more to go off on her endless quest for someone who could give her the sort of loving relationship she was constantly reading about in the pages of *True Romance*.

The unlucky man she chose this time was Richard Morton, who was dead by the following year, having failed all the stringent tests that Nannie applied to every man who crossed her path.

There is no telling how long Nannie Doss might have carried on in this manner, marrying and then killing off her latest husband once she had found him wanting, to say nothing of those she might have murdered merely to keep her hand in control. As it was, the original motivation for getting rid of her husbands must have become blurred with the passage of time. She had been killing off her husbands with such ease and without a single inquest ever having been called for, that murder had become almost second nature with her. She had now reached the stage when any man who was foolish enough to marry her was almost certain to leave the house feet first, however good a husband he turned out to be.

Her fifth and final marriage took place in 1954, when she married fifty-eight-year-old Samuel Doss. In the October of that year he was suddenly taken seriously ill with severe stomach pains and was rushed to hospital in Tulsa. Much to Nanny's consternation, he recovered and returned home, where he found Nannie waiting for him on the doorstep, a huge smile of welcome on her lips.

'Thank heaven you're home safe and sound!' she said, guiding him into the house and through to the living room. She pointed to a large bowl on the table. 'To celebrate your return, I've made a large dish of stewed prunes for dessert.' She gazed at him fondly. 'You like those, don't you, Sam?'

It may have crossed Mr Doss's mind that stewed prunes was hardly the ideal dish to put before a man who had just been pulled back from the brink of death after being suddenly and inexplicably struck down with violent stomach pains. But he said nothing, and dutifully finished off a large helping of the prunes at lunch-time. Within a matter of hours he was back in hospital, where he died the following day.

This time Nannie was not as fortunate as she had been on those previous occasions when her handiwork had passed unnoticed by some overworked local doctor who had always issued the death certificate without question, always noting that the cause of death had been from food poisoning. This time, however, Nannie Doss had to deal with Dr N.Z. Schwelbein, a physician who was quite capable of carrying out an autopsy when he thought it necessary. The day after her husband's death, Dr Schwelbein phoned Nannie. He wasted no time in coming to the point.

'Mrs Doss – I have to tell you that I think an autopsy is necessary to find out the exact cause of your husband's death.' He cleared his throat. 'The stomach pains he was exhibiting during the time he was alive seem to me highly suspicious.'

'If you feel the need, then of course there must be an autopsy,' Nannie agreed promptly. 'After all, what killed him, might kill someone else.'

'It's best to find out for sure,' Dr Schwelbein said, almost apologetically, a little taken aback by Nannie's immediate show of co-operation.

'Of course it is,' Nannie said serenely. 'Good day, Dr Schwelbein.'

Although Nannie Doss seemed to be an unlikely candidate to be brought before a court on a charge of murder, Dr Schwelbein knew that even the most unlikely people could turn out to be murderers. In the case of Nannie, his decision to have an autopsy was governed by his unerring sense that something was extremely wrong about the death of Samuel Doss. If only *one* of the doctors who had examined the corpses of the men, women and children that Nannie Doss had killed had asked for a post mortem, a number of lives might well have been saved.

The autopsy on Samuel Doss revealed that he had been administered enough poison to have killed a dozen men. As soon as this startling piece of information had been passed on to the police, they were calling at Nannie's house within hours. Nannie regarded the two officers standing on her doorstep with wide-eyed surprise. 'Why, what ever brings you two boys here?'

'We'd like you to accompany us to the precinct,' one of them told her. 'We need to ask you some questions about your husband's death.'

'What sort of questions?' Nannie asked innocently.

'That's for the Chief to decide,' one of the officers said. 'We're just here to take you to the precinct.'

'I'll come right away,' Nannie said. She gave them a roguish smile. 'One should always try and help the police wherever possible.'

Down at the precinct, Nannie could not have been more co-operative, though she looked a little taken aback when she was told that she was suspected of murdering her husband. Rallying, she said firmly. 'There has been a terrible mistake. I'm sure it can all be explained.'

'Let's hope so,' the examining officer said.

'You'll see I'm right,' Nannie said confidently. 'Ask all the questions you want, officer. My conscience is clear.' She settled back comfortably in her chair. 'Now tell me what all this is about.'

From then on Nannie Doss more or less took charge of the interview, reducing the police to a helpless silence as she talked endlessly about her life with the late Samuel Doss.

'Mrs Doss,' one of the officers said, when he was finally allowed to get a word in edgeways, 'did you kill your husband?'

'Certainly not,' Nannie said indignantly. 'Sam was a good man. I had no reason to kill him.'

'We happen to think otherwise,' she was told. 'What did your husband have to eat the day before he died?'

'I know we had stewed prunes for dessert,' Nannie said. 'I remember that because I made it as a special treat for Sam when he came back from the hospital.' She smiled fondly as she remembered the late Mr Doss. 'Stewed prunes was one of his favourite dishes.'

Nannie was very much at ease as she sat there, fending off the relentless flow of questions with the same answer – she had a poor memory, and just couldn't remember the answers to all the questions the police kept putting to her.

'I'm sorry. I really do have a terrible memory,' she giggled.

The police hammered away at her for several days, only to be balked at every turn by Nannie's incredibly poor memory.

'What about Richard Morton?' they asked. 'Perhaps you'd like to tell us something about his death.'

'Richard Morton? Never heard of him,' Nannie said decisively.

'You don't remember your previous husband?' one of the detectives said incredulously.

'Oh, *him*,' Nannie sniffed. 'Yes – I was married to him for a while.' It was clear from Nannie's manner she had

had no high regard for Richard Morton.

She was then shown an insurance policy she had taken out in his name. 'I suppose you don't remember this either?'

'Well, I guess I wasn't telling the truth,' Nannie said coyly. Miraculously, considering her poor memory, she remembered the exact amount on the policy. 'That insurance was only for $1500. You can't accuse me of killing him for that small sum.'

It took more hours of intensive grilling before Nannie Doss finally admitted that she had killed Richard Morton and Samuel Doss. Even then, the police did not realize just how busy she had been over the years until her confession was published in all the State's newspapers, and people began phoning in asking questions about Nannie's husbands and relatives who had all died of food poisoning. Realizing they were probably holding a mass killer in custody, the police applied for a whole series of exhumation orders which eventually revealed that *all* the remains contained traces of arsenic. While all this was going on Nannie Doss sat quietly in her cell reading whatever romance magazines she could lay her hands on.

Nannie Doss went on trial in Tulsa charged with killing no fewer than eleven people. She admitted freely to the crimes, but strenuously denied that she had killed them for the insurance money. 'All my husbands were a sad disappointment to me,' she said. 'I had to get rid of them to allow me to look for another husband.' She gave the court-room one of those warm smiles which had endeared her to so many people in the past. 'I killed them because I was looking for the perfect mate.'

'What about the others?' the Prosecutor asked coldly. 'Your mother and your two sisters, for instance?'

Nannie Doss merely shrugged.

Nannie Doss was convicted of mass murder and sent to prison for life, where she died of leukaemia in 1965. She remained a devoted reader of *True Romance* to the last.

MRS MOWRY'S LAST LOVE

Colin Close ('Dr Richard Campbell')

American murder case 1929

Ever since her husband had died ten years before, Mrs Mildred Mowry had been a lonely woman. She had toyed with the idea of marrying again, but having taken a long look at herself in the mirror she had decided against trying to remarry. Who would want a plain, middle-aged Polish lady like me? she had said to herself. She had therefore put out of her mind any thought of marrying again, consoling herself with the knowledge that the years she had spent with her husband had been good years, even though they had been spent in the coal regions of Pennsylvania, where her husband had slaved his life away on the coal face with nothing to show for it at the end, except their house and a life insurance policy which had paid out a few thousand dollars.

Deciding there was no point in leaving the region where all her friends were, Mildred had supplemented her capital by selling the house and taking an apartment for herself in Greenville, where she had begun to take in needlework, to keep herself occupied more than anything else.

Now fifty, she found her thoughts turning once more to marriage. The man who might have me wouldn't be getting much, she told herself. But then I'm not expecting much either. It never even occurred to her that with the nice nest egg she had tucked away in the bank, she had a far more valuable asset than mere good looks.

In July 1928, Mrs Mowry inserted an advertisement in a matrimonial magazine, stating that a widowed fifty-year-old Polish lady was seeking a husband. Rather unwisely, she mentioned she had some six thousand dollars which might be put to good use in a joint business venture if the right man came along.

The advertisement brought an immediate response from a Dr Richard Campbell, who wrote saying that he was a surgeon with a large New York practice, and that he would very much like to meet her. A meeting was arranged, and in due course a well-dressed middle-aged man, with prematurely white hair and wearing a pair of rimless spectacles, arrived at the apartment.

Over a glass of home-made mulberry wine, Dr Campbell told her that his speciality was intestinal surgery. 'You might call me an inside man,' he grinned.

'You mentioned in your letter that you have a large practice in New York,' Mildred prompted him.

'A very large one indeed,' Dr Campbell said gravely. 'Many important people come to see me – including a large number of film stars. I'm treating Tom Mix at this very moment.'

Mrs Mowry was enchanted by the doctor, and was overjoyed when he asked if he might call again. 'I do hope I have no competition,' the doctor said as Mrs Mowry showed him to the door. 'It would not really be surprising if I had – being as you're such an attractive woman.'

'You're the only one,' Mrs Mowry said, blushing.

It was clear from the beginning that Dr Campbell meant business. He checked into one of the local hotels from where he bombarded Mrs Mowry with roses and loving messages. It was all a little too much for Mrs Mowry, who could hardly believe in her good fortune in netting such a catch.

The romance proceeded, with Dr Campbell becoming a regular visitor to the apartment where he was introduced to her two closest friends, Mrs Dodds and Mrs Straub. 'What do you think of him?' Millie asked after he had departed.

'I think you should be careful,' Mrs Straub said. 'You know nothing about him.'

'Nonsense,' Millie said. 'You've only to look at him to see that he's obviously very well off.'

One afternoon when Dr Campbell was at the apartment, the conversation just happened to turn to money. 'My bank pays me three per cent on my savings,' Mildred told him.

'Three per cent!' Dr Campbell choked with anger. 'The bank is cheating you. If you'll allow me to invest your money for you, I'll see to it that it makes much more than that.'

'I don't know,' Mildred said doubtfully. 'I don't like to take chances with what little money I have.'

'You wouldn't be taking any chances, Millie, dear,' Dr Campbell said. '*If* anything should go wrong, I'd make the money up myself. But it's entirely up to you.'

If there had ever been the slightest doubt in Mildred's mind about the intentions of 'Dicky Boy' as she was now given to calling him, her mind was set at rest when he proposed marriage. 'I suggest we both slip quietly away one night without bothering to tell anyone.'

Mildred reluctantly agreed, but before they went she could not resist writing a brief note to Mrs Straub, saying she had eloped with Dr Campbell. She returned some six weeks later in a strangely subdued mood for someone who had recently been married. Her married life so far had not been without its difficulties, she told her friends. As the doctor's flat was being redecorated they had been forced to stay in a small residential hotel in New York. To complicate matters even further the doctor had been called to Hollywood to carry out an operation on Cecil B. DeMille, the famous film director. 'There could be difficulties,' Dr Campbell had told her. 'So it might be some time before I return.'

'There's no sense in wasting money on a room in New York,' Mildred told her friends a little ruefully. 'So we agreed that I should stay here until Dicky Boy gets in touch with me on his return.'

Christmas came and went without a word from Dr Campbell. Finally, in the following February, Mildred announced to Mrs Straub that Dicky Boy had returned to New York and had written to ask her to join him. There was a certain edge to Mildred's voice that made Mrs Straub suspect that Mildred had still heard nothing from Dr Campbell, but was going to look for him. Mrs Straub saw her off on the train, and that was the last time she ever saw her.

She did, however, receive a letter from Mildred telling her that everything was now all right as she had been reunited with Dr Campbell at last. Mrs Straub noticed that the address on the letter was 607 Hudson Street, New York, and not an address in Park Avenue, where the doctor was supposed to have his apartment. She thought this rather strange, and fortunately, as things turned out, decided to keep the letter.

It was soon afterwards that Mrs Straub received a letter that a charred body had been found in a lonely part of the woods in Union County, New Jersey. The body was that of a woman who had been shot through the crown of the head and then set alight after being doused with petrol. The remains had been taken to the city of Elizabeth where they were examined briefly by the city's Public Prosecutor, Abe David. At that time the police often worked closely with the Pinkerton Detective Agency, and Abe David decided that one of their skilled operators had more chance of solving the case than any of his own men. In answer to his call for assistance they sent along William Wagner, the Assistant Superintendent of the New York office.

Wagner's examination of the body and the deductions he made from it were masterly, and would have done credit to the great fictional detective Sherlock Holmes.

'The victim was a middle-aged Slavic woman, probably Polish and living in Pennsylvania,' Wagner told the prosecutor. 'There was probably a new man in her life at the time she died, and she may well have earned her living as a dressmaker, or something like that.'

The Prosecutor looked at him in wonder. 'How did you work all that out?'

'It wasn't too difficult,' Wagner said laconically. 'The victim had high cheek bones, a notable characteristic of the Slavic races. The shoes were made by the Friedman Shelby Shoe Company of St Louis, who have always done a great deal of business in the Pennsylvania mining towns for years. Most of the Slavs who work in that area are Poles. She had done a lot of repairs on her dress which shows a certain amount of highly skilled needlework.'

'And what about the new man in her life?'

'The jewellery she was wearing was all cheap stuff, but it was all new as far as I could make out. All that new jewellery seems to indicate that she had started making herself look attractive to some man.'

'Now all you've got to do is to find out who she was,' the Prosecutor smiled.

'That shouldn't be too difficult,' Wagner said confidently.

Convinced that the dead woman had come from the mining area of Pennsylvania, Wagner made a tour of the region, talking to the local police and distributing posters around each town, asking for information on anyone who had recently disappeared. His search produced nothing, and he returned to his office in New Jersey, wondering if his reasoning had been badly flawed.

No sooner had he returned to his office than he received a phone call from Greenville, where he had displayed a number of posters in prominent positions around the town. The phone call was from the local police chief who told him that he had been visited by two women who claimed they might be able to tell him something about the missing woman. The two women were Mrs Dodds and Mrs Straub.

'Send them up here,' Wagner told the police chief.

'Maybe they can identify the body.'

The two ladies went to New Jersey where Wagner showed them the charred remains which had been lying in the morgue icebox all this time. Although barely recognizable, they were both still able to identify the dead woman as being Mildred Mowry. Afterwards, Wagner took the two badly shocked women to his office, where Mrs Straub told him of Mildred's marriage to Dr Campbell and the way in which she had suddenly dropped from sight after her return to New York. Mrs Straub showed him Mildred's letter.

'This is the last time I heard from her,' Mrs Straub told him.

When Wagner checked the address on the letter it turned out to be a YWCA which Mildred had left only the day before her torched body had been found in the woods. 'I remember the lady,' the receptionist told him. 'She stayed here for some weeks, and most of that time she seemed in a pretty depressed state of mind. On the day she left she was quite different. It was as if a great weight had been lifted off her mind.'

Everything was now beginning to fall into place. The way that Wagner saw it, Dr Campbell had married poor Mildred and had put her into the residential hotel in New York until he got hold of her money, when he had gradually eased himself out of her life, making his visits to the hotel more and more infrequent, until he vanished for good with the excuse that he had been called to Hollywood to carry out the operation on Cecil B. DeMille. Mildred had returned home and spent several months waiting for him to reappear before finally going off to New York to seek him out. While she had been staying at the YWCA, she had obviously found him, only to be killed for her trouble.

Wagner sighed. The story was an all too familiar one: the plain and trusting middle-aged woman who had been cheated out of her savings by some callous con man. Only this time murder had been added to the crime.

Who *was* Campbell? Wagner wondered. Certainly not a well-known surgeon living at a Park Avenue address. More to the point, where *had* he lived? Wagner got on the phone to the police chief in Greenville and asked for a search to be carried out in Mildred Mowry's flat to see if any correspondence from the bogus doctor was left lying around. The search produced two addresses in New York – both of which turned out to belong to mail-receiving services.

Having come to a blind alley with that line of enquiry, Wagner began to wonder where they had been married. Where would a man who was probably already married sneak off to in the night to make a bigamous marriage without too many questions being asked? He decided that it was probably in Elkton in Maryland, a place that was akin to Britain's Gretna Green, where runaway couples had been able to get married at any time of the day. Moreover, it was only a few hours' distance from Greenville.

For once Wagner was in luck. Dr Campbell and Mildred had indeed been married in Elkton. The address of the bridegroom had been given as 3,700 Yosemite Street, Baltimore. Wagner went there in high hopes – only to find that the house had been pulled down years ago and was now a vacant lot.

Realizing that Campbell must have known the area well to pick a vacant lot as his address, Wagner then proceeded to canvas the area around Yosemite Street. He was beginning to lose hope when he came upon a landlord who had rented an apartment to a man answering to Campbell's description. 'You must be talking about Dr Colin Close,' the landlord said. 'I've no idea where he moved on from here.'

It occurred to Wagner that Colin Close might be Dr Campbell's real name, and that he might have a criminal record somewhere under that name. As Pinkerton had agents throughout the United States, it wasn't too difficult

for Wagner to get access to the police records in all the
major cities. Sure enough, the police in Chicago had a
thick file on a man under that name.

Colin Close had studied medicine as a young man, only
to abandon it in favour of petty crime which had led to a
sentence in Fulsom Prison. After he had been released he
had come to New York, where he had held a number of
jobs until he had been sent to Sing Sing for swindling his
employers. He had next turned up in Omaha with an
attaché case full of fake credentials which had landed him
a plum job as educational director for the Union Pacific
Railroad. After simultaneously getting engaged to five
girls, he had fled to Chicago where he had become a
public relations officer specializing in promoting housing
developments. From then on he must have kept himself
on the right side of the law as there was no further record
of his activities for the last nine years.

Knowing that Close had specialized in promoting
housing developments, Wagner began phoning around the
companies in New Jersey who dealt with such operations.
Finally he found one with a promotion expert named
Richard Campbell, who answered the description of the
man that Wagner was seeking. Wagner wrote down his
address and then replaced the receiver. He stared blankly
at the wall. Campbell lived in an apartment around the
corner from the morgue where the body of Mildred
Mowry had been taken.

Wagner went to the apartment, where he found that
Campbell had a wife and two children. Stunned at what
Wagner had to tell her, his wife told him that she was
expecting her husband back that evening. 'I don't understand it,' she cried. 'He has always been such a devoted
husband.'

When Campbell returned that evening, Wagner and the
police from Elizabeth were waiting for him. Faced with
this formidable array of representatives of the law, Campbell readily confessed. 'She was waiting for me when I

went to collect my mail from one of the addresses I gave her,' he said. 'I sent her back to the YWCA to collect her things while I went off and got myself a gun. I picked her up later and drove her around all day, pretending that I was visiting patients. When it was dark and she was beginning to dose off, I shot her.'

Wagner asked him something that had been puzzling him. 'How come you shot her through the crown of her head?'

'I didn't want any bloodstains or a bullet in my car.'

'Take him away,' Wagner said in disgust.

A year later Campbell was sent to the electric chair in Trenton.

A RESPECTABLE HOUSEHOLD

Alma Rattenbury and George Stoner

English murder case 1935

The Rattenbury-Stoner murder took place in the 1930s, a vintage decade for murder cases in Britain. Why then is this case remembered more than any other that occurred during this period, with the exception of the equally famous Thompson-Bywaters case, which was to cast a long shadow over the trial of Alma Rattenbury and George Stoner, both accused of the murder of Alma's husband, Francis Rattenbury?

Two things have kept this case firmly in the mind of the public, even though the murder took place more than fifty years ago. Firstly, it was a *crime passionnel* which had been committed without a thought to the possible consequences, and it had been carried out behind the lace curtains of an outwardly respectable-looking bungalow in Bournemouth, a seaside resort known more for being a place to retire to than for its crime rate. Secondly, there was the tragic circumstance of Alma Rattenbury's death, which took on the appearance of a Greek tragedy as she left this world by plunging a dagger through her body six times before she finally expired on the lonely river bank where she had decided to end it all.

Alma Rattenbury's life was a disastrous one, though to begin with everything seemed to be in her favour. Born in British Columbia in 1895, she grew up to become an extremely attractive young girl with a talent for music. She was educated in Toronto, and by the time she was seventeen she was already playing with the Toronto Symphony Orchestra. After the entire family had moved to Vancouver, she met and fell in love with Caldon Dolling, who ran an estate agent's business in the city. The couple were married in

1914, immediately prior to the outbreak of war, when Dolling immediately joined the Royal Welch Fusiliers. Their idyllic marriage lasted until 1916, when Dolling was killed in action. Grief-stricken, Alma immediately joined a Scottish nursing unit and went to France, where she was wounded twice and was eventually awarded the Croix de Guerre with Star and Palm by the French government.

After the war she settled in London where she met Compton Pakenham, who had served as an officer on the Western Front. Although he was married when they first met, he immediately applied for a divorce, which in those days was not as easy to obtain as it is now. Alma was named as the other woman in the divorce suit, and after a great deal of difficulty Pakenham obtained his decree nisi in 1921. Soon after he had married Alma, Pakenham managed to get a job as a professor at an American university, and for a while Alma and her husband lived in the United States.

The marriage turned sour, and Alma returned with her small son to Vancouver, where she resumed her musical career. It was while she was in Vancouver that she met Francis Rattenbury, a well-known architect in Canada and then at the peak of his career. Although he was nearly thirty years older than she was, Alma took an instant liking to him; he was kind and thoughtful, and unlike Pakenham who had become something of a waster, he seemed a reliable person on whom she could lean after two unhappy marriages. Whether she actually loved him was another matter.

There was only one impediment to them marrying. Rattenbury already had a wife, a situation which Rattenbury immediately tried to rectify by applying for a divorce. After a great deal of unpleasantness, in which Alma was once again cited as the other woman, the divorce came through in 1925.

By 1929, Alma had given Rattenbury a son whom they named John, but her husband had become bitter over the way they had been shunned by his erstwhile friends and colleagues. It was at this stage that Rattenbury decided he would like to spend the rest of his days in England. As it turned out, it was to prove to be the biggest mistake of his life.

When Alma and her husband eventually settled in a house named the Villa Madeira in Bournemouth, Rattenbury was already beginning to look older than his years and had begun to drink heavily. Worse still, as far as Alma was concerned, he had become impotent.

The future now looked bleak for them both. Rattenbury was now more or less retired and on a limited income, while all that Alma had to look forward to was watching her looks fade while she waited for the time when she would become a widow with nothing to do except spend her final years taking aimless walks along the Bournemouth sea front.

To make matters worse, Francis Rattenbury had become mean with his money, claiming that they had to count the pennies to keep abreast of the household bills that kept coming in. To be fair to him, he was very conscious of the fact that his still attractive wife was becoming bored and frustrated with her humdrum life in Bournemouth, and he encouraged her to try her hand at composing, something she had never attempted before. He was so pleased with her efforts that he took some of her work to London and did the rounds of the music publishers, but with little success until he visited Keith Prowse, who agreed to publish some of her songs and, moreover, offered to introduce her to Frank Titterton, a well-known tenor during the 1930s. Alma met Titterton and he eventually recorded and sang some of her songs. Once more Alma seemed to have a purpose in life. She was now travelling to London regularly and mixing once more in musical circles, often meeting her new-found friends for lunch or dinner at the Mayfair Hotel – thanks mainly to Francis Rattenbury who had made it all possible.

Although Titterton become a firm friend of the Rattenburys, and did all he could to further Alma's musical career, it never really took off, and it was not long before the trips to London began to cease, except for the odd occasion when she had lunch with Titterton. It was not enough, and Alma began to drink heavily, as did her husband, who had become almost a bottle-a-day man and was invariably dead drunk by nightfall.

This depressing state of affairs lasted until 1934, with Francis Rattenbury now becoming quite impossible to live with. When he was in one of his more ugly moods, Alma turned to the housekeeper, Irene Riggs, who had joined the family when they had first come to the Villa Madeira. Irene became more of a friend and confidante than a housekeeper, and was privy to much that was going on in the household.

In September that year, Alma suddenly decided to hire someone who could drive the children to school and act as a general handyman about the house, activities which her husband was now quite incapable of carrying out. Irene was opposed to the idea, not wishing to see her unique role in the house being threatened in any way. In order to mollify her, Alma decided to choose someone younger than she had originally planned.

On 23 September 1934, the following advertisement appeared in the *Bournemouth Daily Echo*:

> Willing lad wanted, 14-18, for housework. Scout-trained preferred. Apply 11 – 12, 8 – 9, 5 Manor Road, Bournemouth.

Two young men applied for the job. One of them was George Stoner, who got the job as soon as Alma learned that he could drive a car. The Driving Test had only come into force in June of that year and still did not apply to anyone who could already drive, therefore his age was immaterial. His starting salary was £1 a week.

Stoner was a pleasant-faced, uncomplicated youth who at twenty-one never drank and had no experience with girls, let alone older women such as his attractive employer who was old enough to be his mother. To begin with, his relationship with Alma was very much that of an employee who would never have dreamed of making advances to his employer, while Alma's attitude was little different, except that she was grateful to have him around to take her shopping and ferry the children backwards and forwards to school.

What changed this formal state of affairs is something quite difficult to ascertain, but more likely than not, intimacy first took place when Stoner drove Alma and Irene Riggs to Oxford on a shopping expedition. They all stayed the night at the Randolph Hotel, where Alma probably crept into his bed one night while Irene lay asleep in another room.

Perhaps only the young who have just experienced their first love affair can fully appreciate just how much Stoner was overwhelmed by his experience with this beautiful woman. Passion, to those for whom all passion is spent, is difficult to describe. The sort of sudden, passionate love that Stoner had for Alma Rattenbury is something that most of us are fortunate enough never to know, for in its wake it brings the deadly sin of jealousy that in some cases, can lead to murder – as it did with George Stoner.

Stoner had been brought up in a working-class background where a strict moral code generally prevailed in the 1930s. He was therefore unhappy at first that he had betrayed a man who had done him no harm. Alma brushed aside these scruples by telling him that she had not had sex with her husband for years, who was long past caring what she did with anyone as long as a whisky bottle was always readily available.

By March 1935 Stoner's scruples were gone. He became vain and demanding, and above all, he was now insanely jealous of Francis Rattenbury. By then, Irene had become aware of what was going on, but was in no position to restrain Alma, who had become completely besotted with Stoner.

On Monday 19 March, Alma asked her husband for £250, using the excuse that she wanted the money for a minor operation on her glands, which had become badly infected. Rattenbury had jibbed a little at the expense, but had given her the money, and Alma went off with Stoner, saying that she would put him up at an hotel until she came out of the hospital, when Stoner would bring her home. Irene Riggs watched them go, her resentment now close to boiling point.

Alma and Stoner stayed at the Kensington Palace Hotel for four days. As soon as they were settled in, Alma took Stoner on a series of shopping expeditions and fitted him up with a complete wardrobe of new and expensive clothes. All this high living inflated Stoner's self-esteem still further, so that he began more than ever to resent Rattenbury being around and preventing him from having Alma all to himself.

The whole unhappy business came to a head when Alma and Stoner returned home to find Rattenbury in such a depressed state of mind that he did not even ask how the operation had gone. Seeing that her husband was in one of his many suicidal moods, Alma suggested that they should drive to Bridport, where they could spend the night. 'Stoner will drive us,' she told her husband.

Stoner had no intention of doing any such thing. After having spent four days living in a style to which he had never been accustomed, with servants and shop assistants answering his every beck and call and addressing him as sir, he bitterly resented having to revert to his role of chauffeur and handyman to the Rattenburys. More than ever, his resentment was directed at Rattenbury, who had always treated him more as an equal than a servant, often playing cards with him and generally treating him almost as a member of the family. Stoner's resentment was such that he chose to forget Rattenbury's kindness. In a fit of insane jealousy he produced an air pistol when Rattenbury was out of the room, and brandishing it in Alma's face, threatened to shoot her if she went to Bridport with her husband.

'I know why you're going,' he told her. 'Once you're in Bridport and out of my sight, you're going to sleep with your husband.'

This was quite obviously untrue, and Stoner must have known it, and the incident might have passed without any more trouble if Alma had not made it quite clear that she had every intention of not giving in to Stoner, who went off into the night muttering threats under his breath as he went.

On that fateful evening of 24 March, Stoner made an unexpected visit to the home of his grandparents who lived nearby. He asked them if they had a wooden mallet he could borrow as he needed it to drive in the pegs of a small tent he was putting up in the grounds of the Villa Madeira. His grandfather was able to produce a mallet, and Stoner went away with it shortly afterwards.

Meanwhile, back at the Villa Madeira, Alma was trying to keep her husband's mind occupied by playing cards with him. By then, Rattenbury had already been at the whisky bottle and was beginning to doze over his cards. When she saw that he had finally fallen asleep, Alma went quietly up to her room and began to pack for the trip to Bridport next morning.

Irene Riggs came home about 10.15 that evening and noted nothing unusual, though she was surprised to suddenly come across Stoner looking over the bannisters at the top of the stairs. 'What's the matter?' she asked.

'Nothing,' Stoner said. 'I was just looking to see if all the lights were out.'

Later that evening, when Alma had just retired to bed, Stoner came into her room. 'You won't be going to Bridport,' he told her. He was shaking and looking very upset.

'What ever is the matter, darling?' Alma asked him.

'I'm in terrible trouble,' Stoner said. He sat on the edge of the bed and buried his head in his hands. 'I've just hit your husband over the head with a mallet.' He added tearfully, 'I only did it to stop you going to Bridport together.'

Now thoroughly alarmed, Alma made for the door. 'I must go to him.'

'Please don't go down there,' Stoner pleaded. 'The sight will only upset you.'

Ignoring him, Alma ran out of the room and went downstairs where she had last seen Rattenbury lying in his chair in a drunken stupor. He was still in his chair, but now blood was flowing copiously from his head and running down his clothes in rivulets to the floor, and forming a pool that was slowly seeping into the carpet. Faced with this terrible sight, Alma let out a piercing scream which brought Irene Riggs running downstairs and into the room where she was brought up short by the sight of Francis Rattenbury lying slumped in his chair with blood pouring from his head. Seeing that Alma was in no state to deal with anything, Irene took charge of the situation. First, she phoned their local GP, Dr O'Donnell, and then she packed Stoner off to stay with his parents for the night. She was still vainly trying to comfort Alma when Dr O'Donnell arrived. Seeing that Rattenbury was still alive, he immediately telephoned the hospital for an ambulance and someone more qualified than himself to examine Rattenbury's head wounds. Afterwards he phoned the local police and told them what had happened.

In due course, the ambulance arrived with a surgeon who briefly examined Rattenbury before taking him away in an ambulance. No sooner had they gone than the police arrived, led by Inspector Mills. By this time Alma was hopelessly drunk, after taking frequent swigs at the whisky bottle that stood on the table beside Rattenbury. Desperately clinging on to the remnants of her awareness of what had happened, she tried to take the blame for the murder. 'I did it,' she told Inspector Mills. 'My husband had lived too long. I did it with a mallet.' She then proceeded to make advances on Bagwell, the station sergeant who had taken Dr O'Donnell's call. When she tried to kiss Bagwell, he beat a hasty retreat into the garden. Seeing that the situation was in danger of taking on the air of a stage farce, with Alma reeling drunkenly around the room while Bagwell watched apprehensively through the window, Irene made a valiant attempt to control her mistress by putting her in a chair and then sitting on her.

It was now 3.30 in the morning, and it was then that Dr O'Donnell decided that enough was enough, and that as Mrs Rattenbury now had no clear idea of what was going on, he took her up to her bedroom, where he administered half a grain of morphia. He then went downstairs again and was having a few words with the inspector when Mrs Rattenbury bounced into the room again, bright as a cricket, though all too obviously still blind drunk. Inspector Mills was about to question her when he was interrupted by Dr O'Donnell. 'Mrs Rattenbury is in no state to be questioned,' he told Inspector Mills firmly. 'Just look at her condition, man. She is full of whisky and I have just given her a large dose of morphia. She must be put to bed at once!' He took her upstairs again, and this time Mrs Rattenbury stayed in her bed and soon fell into a heavy, drugged sleep. The good doctor who had stood no nonsense from the police then ushered them out of the house and then went home himself. It had been a night that neither the police nor Dr O'Donnell were to forget for a long time.

At six o'clock the next morning Detective Inspector William Carter from the Criminal Investigation Department arrived at the house. He found Mrs Rattenbury awake, but still in no condition to be questioned. With the formidable Dr O'Donnell no longer present, the Inspector wasted no time in getting Mrs Rattenbury fit enough to answer some questions. Irene Riggs was sent off to make some coffee while he telephoned the police station to ask for a policewoman to come round at once in order to give Mrs Rattenbury a bath, which he hoped would bring her back to some kind of normality. When Alma finally came downstairs she was pale and shaky, but clearly now quite able to answer the Inspector's questions.

'Would you tell me exactly what occurred last night?' Her statement, written down by Inspector Carter in his notebook, was as follows:

About 9 PM on the 24th March I was playing cards with my husband when he dared me to kill him, as he wanted to die. I picked up a mallet and he then said: 'You have not got the guts to do it.' I then hit him with the mallet. I hid the mallet outside. I would have shot him if I had a gun.

At this stage Alma had no other thought than to save her
lover – even at the expense of her own life. The fact that the
statement was obviously preposterous was ignored by
Inspector Carter, who had taken it down without comment.
He did not ask, for instance, how it was that Alma just
happened to have a mallet handy beside her chair to knock
in Mr Rattenbury's head. Instead, he then went to take a
statement from Stoner, who had been brought back to the
house. Knowing nothing of Alma's 'confession' Stoner
merely filled in a few details about his own position in the
household, and that he had been aroused from his bed by
Mrs Rattenbury screaming, when he had gone down to find
Mr Rattenbury lying slumped in his chair, with blood
pouring from his head. Inspector Carter then went back to
Alma and charged her with the attempted murder of her
husband. As she left in the company of the police inspector,
she passed Irene Riggs standing in the passage and made the
odd remark: 'Don't make fools of yourselves.'

'You have got yourself into this trouble by talking too
much,' Stoner muttered as she went out of the door.

On 28 March Francis Rattenbury died in hospital. By
then Stoner had learned of Alma's confession. Although the
charge was now one of murder, Stoner immediately
confessed to Irene and told her he was going to give
himself up. Irene never gave him the chance. She phoned the
police at once, and by the evening Stoner had been arrested
and charged with the murder of Francis Rattenbury.

One of the edifying aspects of this case was the
unswerving determination of Alma and Stoner to shoulder
the blame. It was not until Alma's lawyers told her to
reconsider her statement and change her plea to one of
not guilty for the sake of her children that she withdrew
her original statement to the police.

One thing remains unexplained to this day, and has never
been touched on in any detail except by Sir David Napley
in his excellent book *Murder at the Villa Madeira*, and that
is the reason why Alma Rattenbury never supplied the

funds to provide Stoner with a first-class defence lawyer, when she was able to get herself one of the best in the land at the time. Stoner had to rely on the Poor Prisoner's Defence Act first introduced in 1930, and which had only limited funds for a defence. J.D. Caswell was chosen to defend him, a more than able lawyer but with no great flair for advocacy, and who was to be hampered considerably by Stoner who was determined to involve Alma as little as possible.

The trial of Alma Rattenbury and George Stoner began at the Old Bailey on 27 May 1935. As usual, the case had been given more than its fair share of coverage by the press, which had concentrated its interest more on Alma Rattenbury than Stoner, with the result that the court-room was made up mostly of women who were curious to see Mrs Rattenbury in the flesh. In many of their minds must have been the memory of the Edith Thompson-Frederick Bywaters case, where both had been hanged because the judge had laid undue stress on their adultery. In some ways that case and this one were not dissimilar, in that the murder of a husband and a pair of guilty lovers were the centrepiece of the trial. Was the same thing going to happen this time? many wondered.

The fact that Mr Justice Humphreys was presiding over the case was not entirely reassuring to those who knew anything about him either. Although he was a very fair judge, he had a very stern moral code when it came to dealing with people who had committed adultery. Would he condemn Mrs Rattenbury and Stoner on those grounds as Mr Justice Spearman had done in the Thompson-Bywaters case?

As soon as the trial got under way it soon became clear that this was not to be so. Throughout the whole trial Mr Justice Humphreys behaved with scrupulous fairness, as did the prosecution led by Mr Croom-Johnson, KC, who gave the defence every opportunity to present its case as fairly as possible, and was surprisingly restrained when dealing with Mrs Rattenbury. At only one point did the judge betray a somewhat Victorian attitude, and that was in his summing up, when he said of Mrs Rattenbury, 'You cannot have any feelings except of disgust for her.' For a few moments only it seemed as if the Old Bailey had once more become a court of morals.

On 31 May, the jury was sent out to consider its verdict. They returned in less than an hour with their decision. Alma Rattenbury had been found not guilty, and Stoner found guilty, but with an added rider recommending him to mercy.

'Oh, no,' Alma moaned, casting an anguished look at Stoner, before the wardress guided her from the dock. White-faced, Stoner listened in silence while Justice Humphreys sentenced him to death. Then he turned away abruptly and was led back to his cell.

Alma Rattenbury left the court the same day and was taken to a nursing home. She stayed there for four days, in which time she saw her friend Irene Riggs, and told her that when she died she wanted pink flowers at her funeral. Although Irene was worried by the remark, she put it down to Alma's still highly distressed state of mind.

On Wednesday of that week, Alma took herself off to another nursing home in Bayswater, from where she wrote a letter to Stoner, and another to one of her friends, in which she expressed the conviction that Stoner would be reprieved. The next day her feeling of hope must have changed to a mood of black depression, for she suddenly left the nursing home and took a train to Christchurch, where she stabbed herself to death.

Ironically, three weeks after her death, Stoner was reprieved.